FOX &

RABBiT

FOX &
CELEBRATE

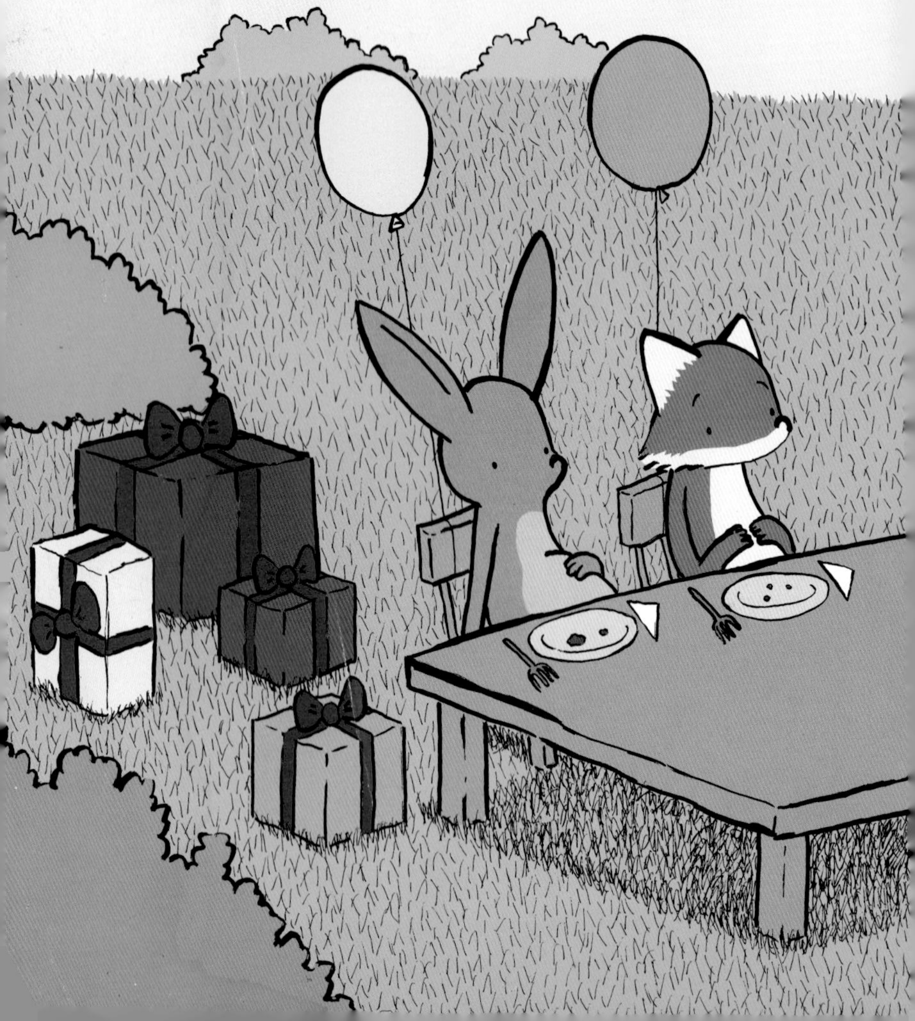

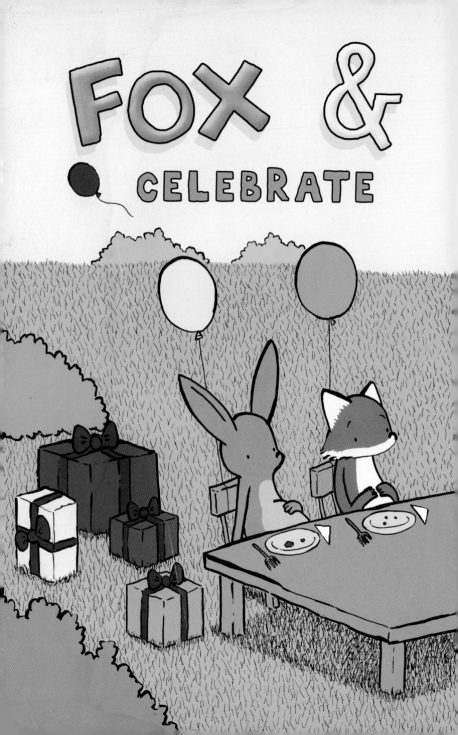

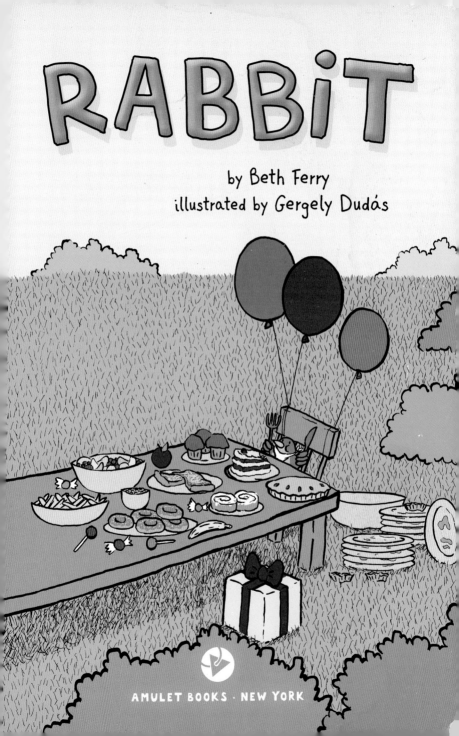

RABBiT

by Beth Ferry
illustrated by Gergely Dudás

AMULET BOOKS · NEW YORK

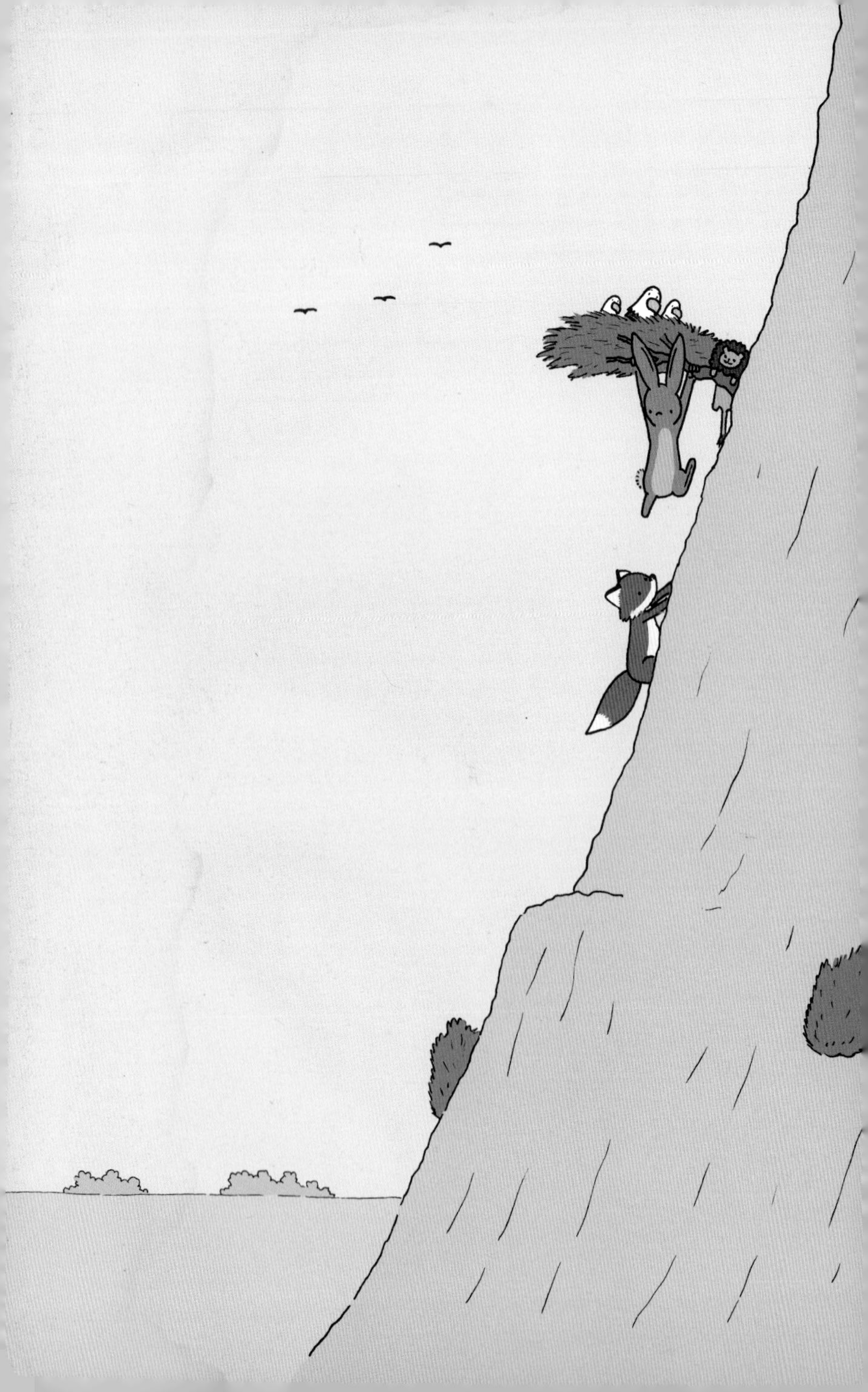

CONTENTS

STORY ONE

FIX, FUSS & FLIES

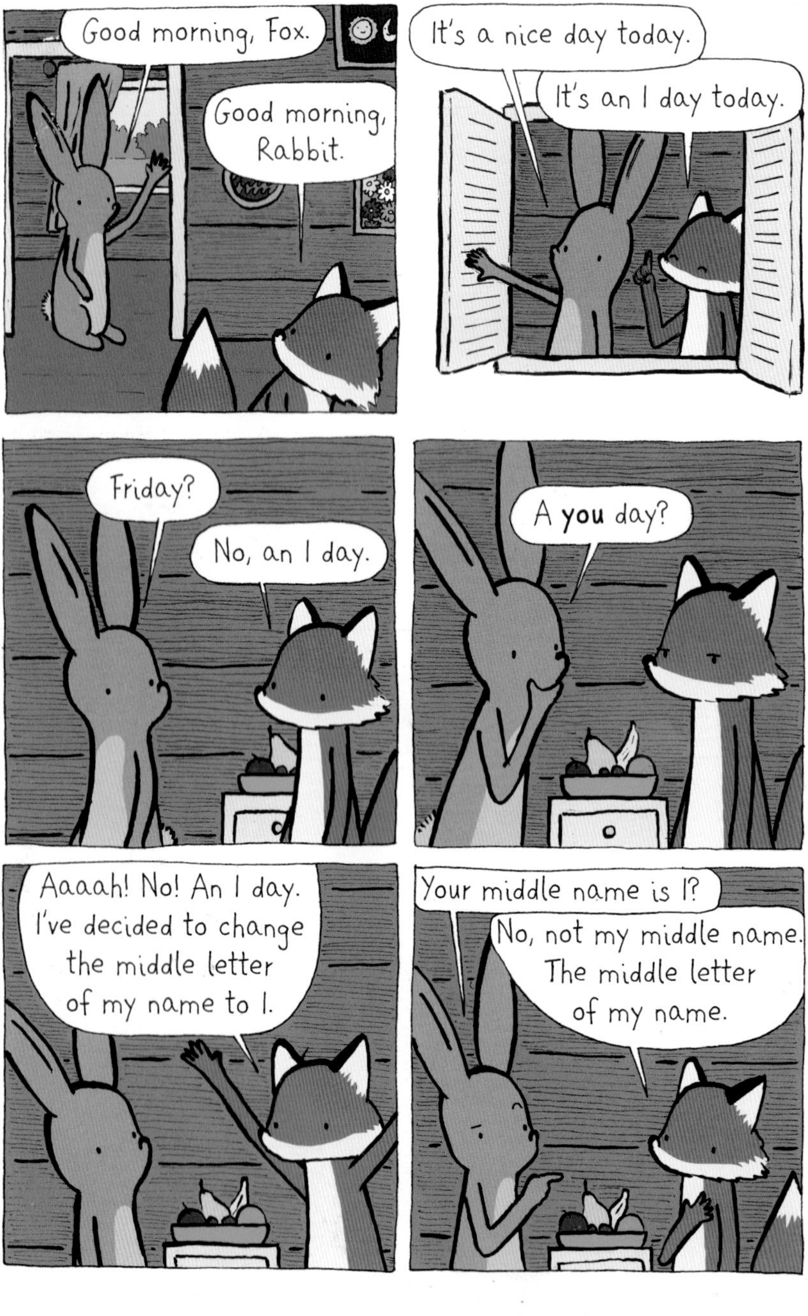
Good morning, Fox.
Good morning, Rabbit.
It's a nice day today.
It's an I day today.
Friday?
No, an I day.
A **you** day?
Aaaah! No! An I day. I've decided to change the middle letter of my name to I.
Your middle name is I?
No, not my middle name. The middle letter of my name.

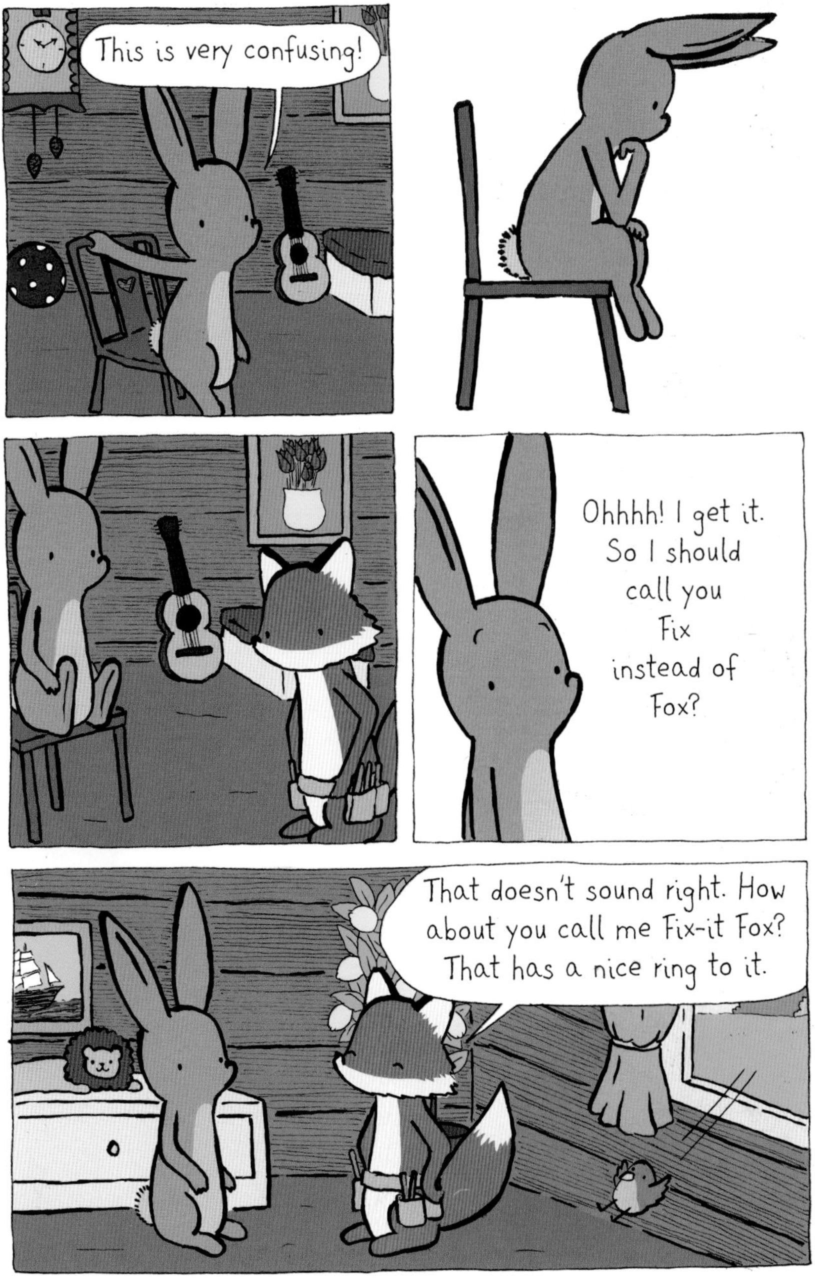
This is very confusing!
Ohhhh! I get it. So I should call you Fix instead of Fox?
That doesn't sound right. How about you call me Fix-it Fox? That has a nice ring to it.

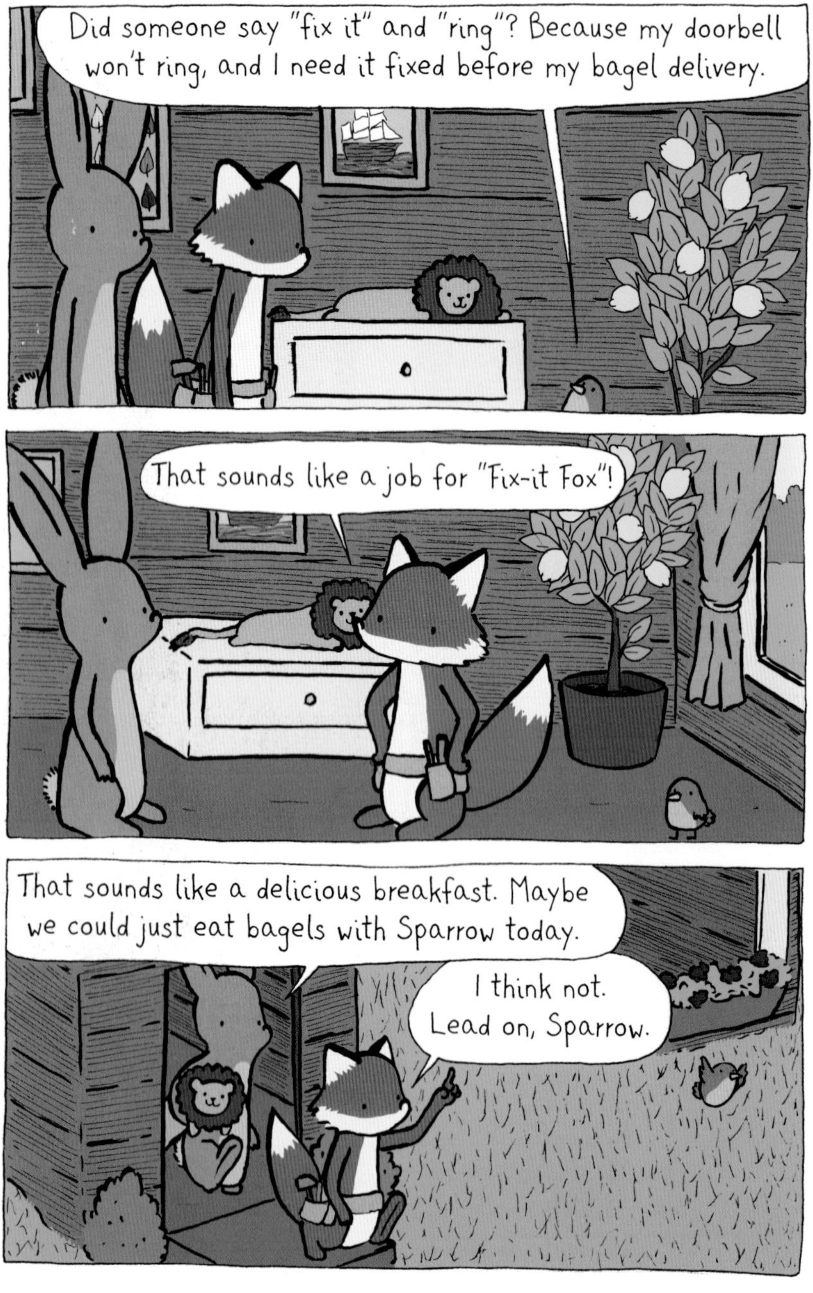
Did someone say "fix it" and "ring"? Because my doorbell won't ring, and I need it fixed before my bagel delivery.
That sounds like a job for "Fix-it Fox"!
That sounds like a delicious breakfast. Maybe we could just eat bagels with Sparrow today.
I think not. Lead on, Sparrow.

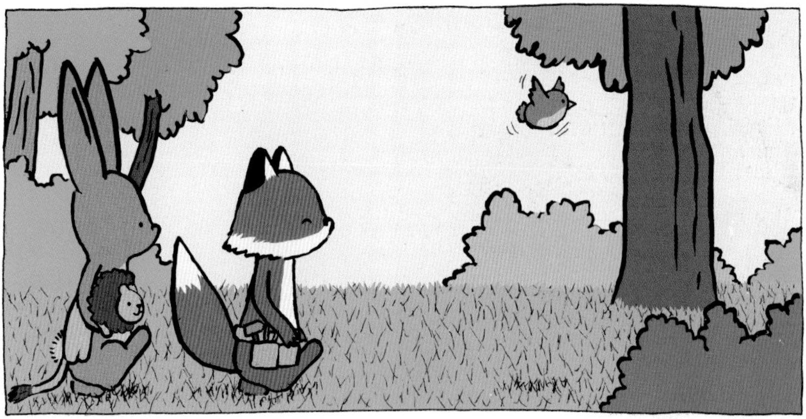

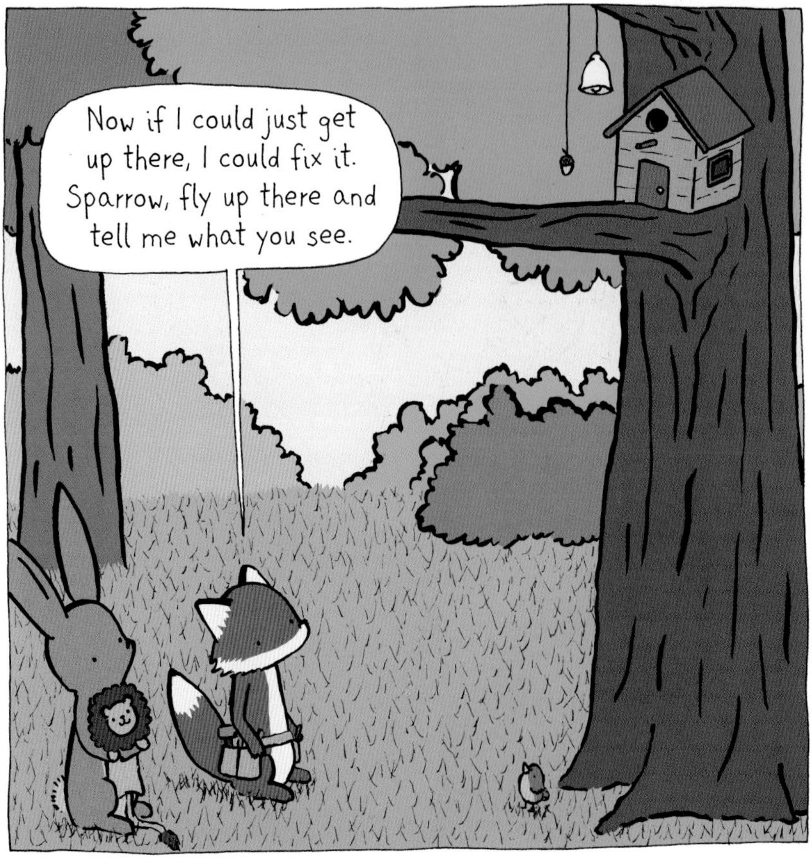
Now if I could just get up there, I could fix it. Sparrow, fly up there and tell me what you see.

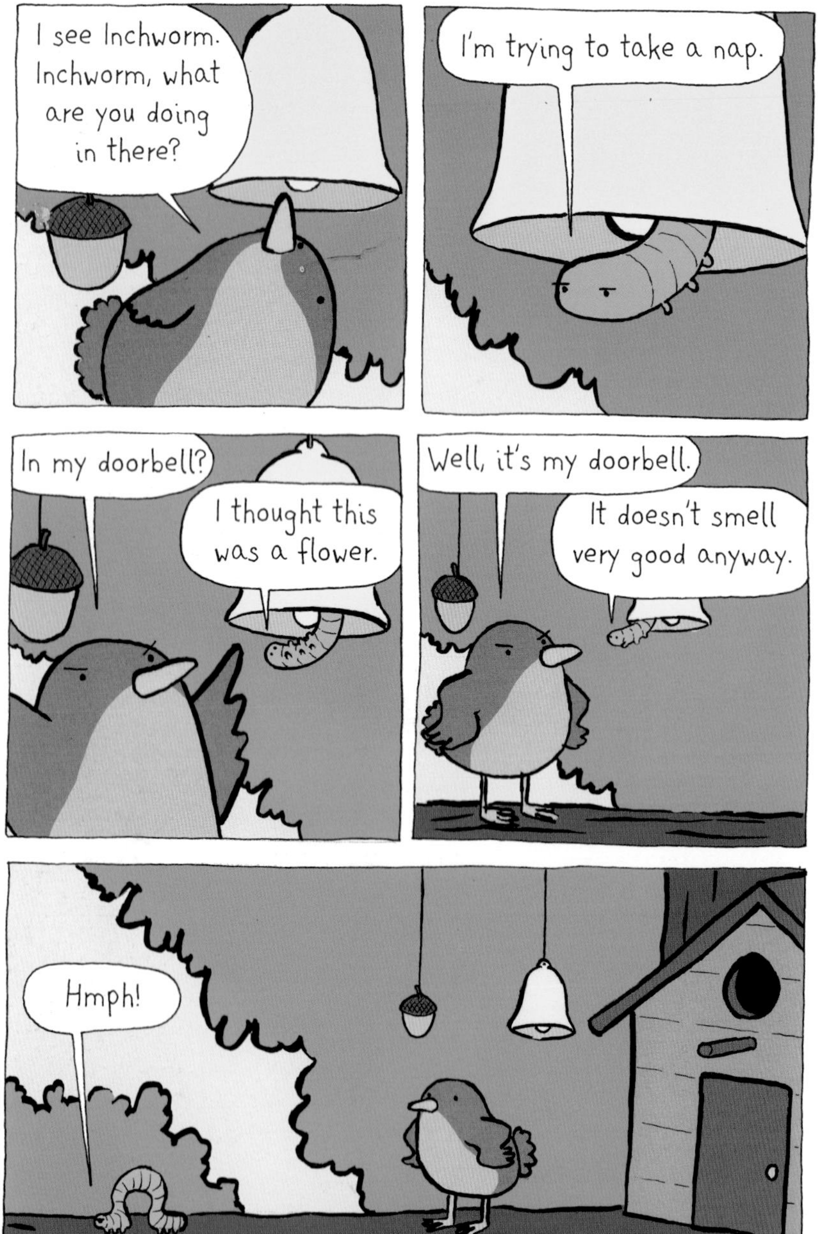
I see Inchworm. Inchworm, what are you doing in there?
I'm trying to take a nap.
In my doorbell?
I thought this was a flower.
Well, it's my doorbell.
It doesn't smell very good anyway.
Hmph!

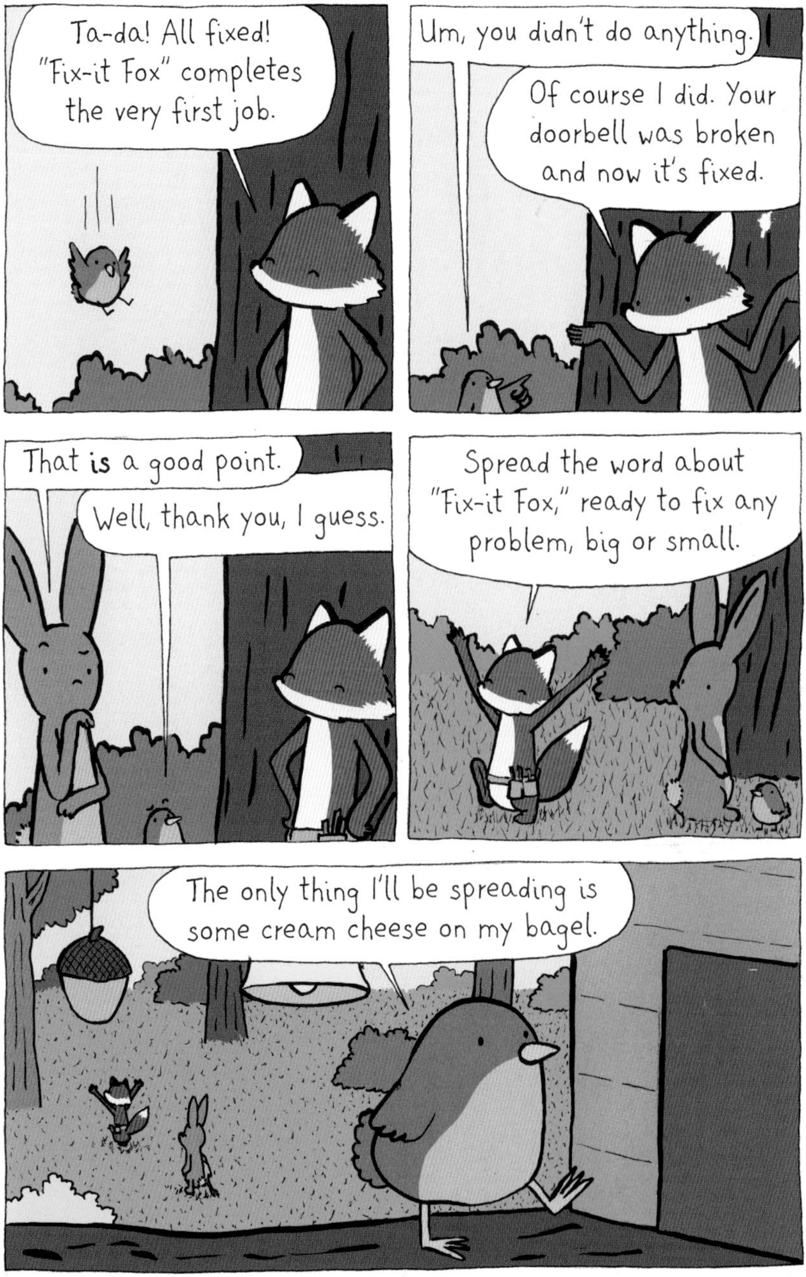
Ta-da! All fixed! "Fix-it Fox" completes the very first job.
Um, you didn't do anything.
Of course I did. Your doorbell was broken and now it's fixed.
That **is** a good point.
Well, thank you, I guess.
Spread the word about "Fix-it Fox," ready to fix any problem, big or small.
The only thing I'll be spreading is some cream cheese on my bagel.

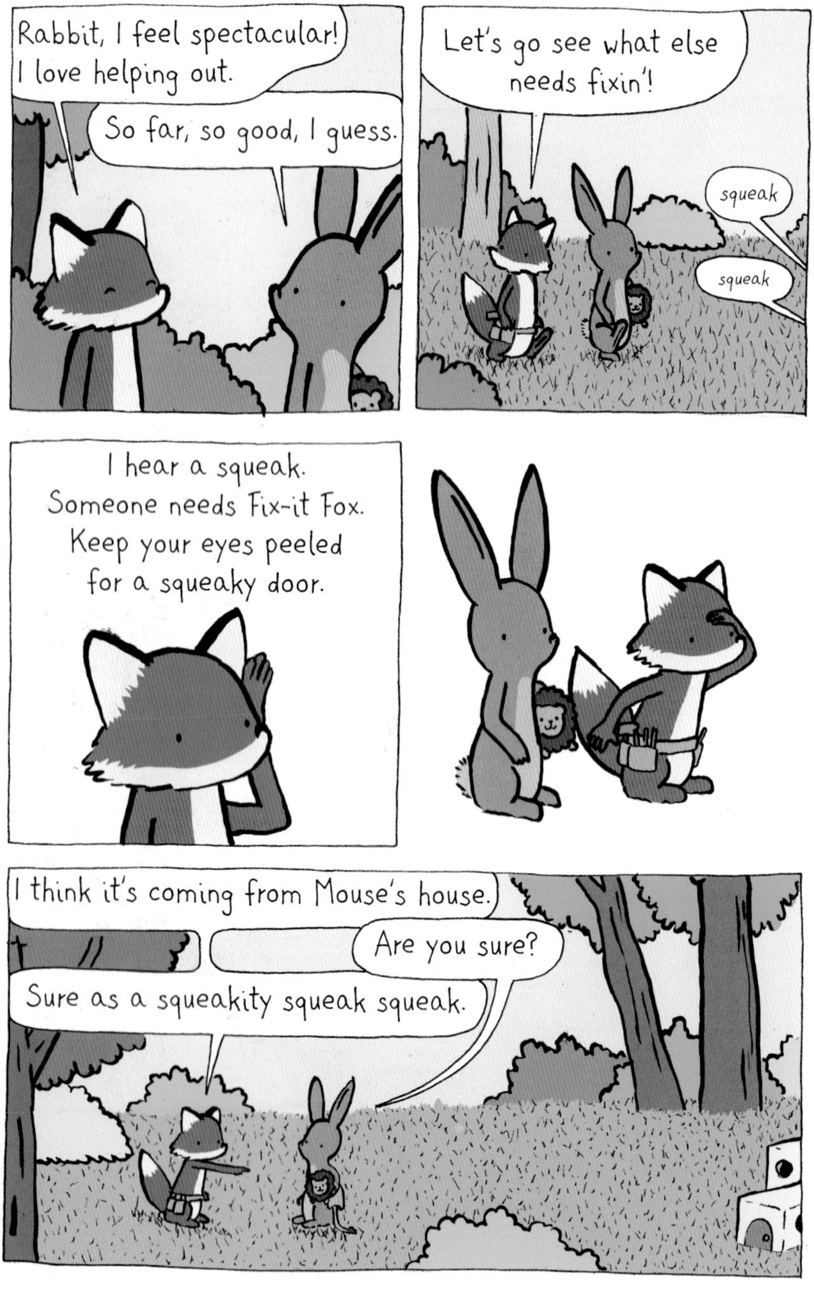
Rabbit, I feel spectacular! I love helping out.
So far, so good, I guess.
Let's go see what else needs fixin'!
squeak
squeak
I hear a squeak. Someone needs Fix-it Fox. Keep your eyes peeled for a squeaky door.
I think it's coming from Mouse's house.
Are you sure?
Sure as a squeakity squeak squeak.

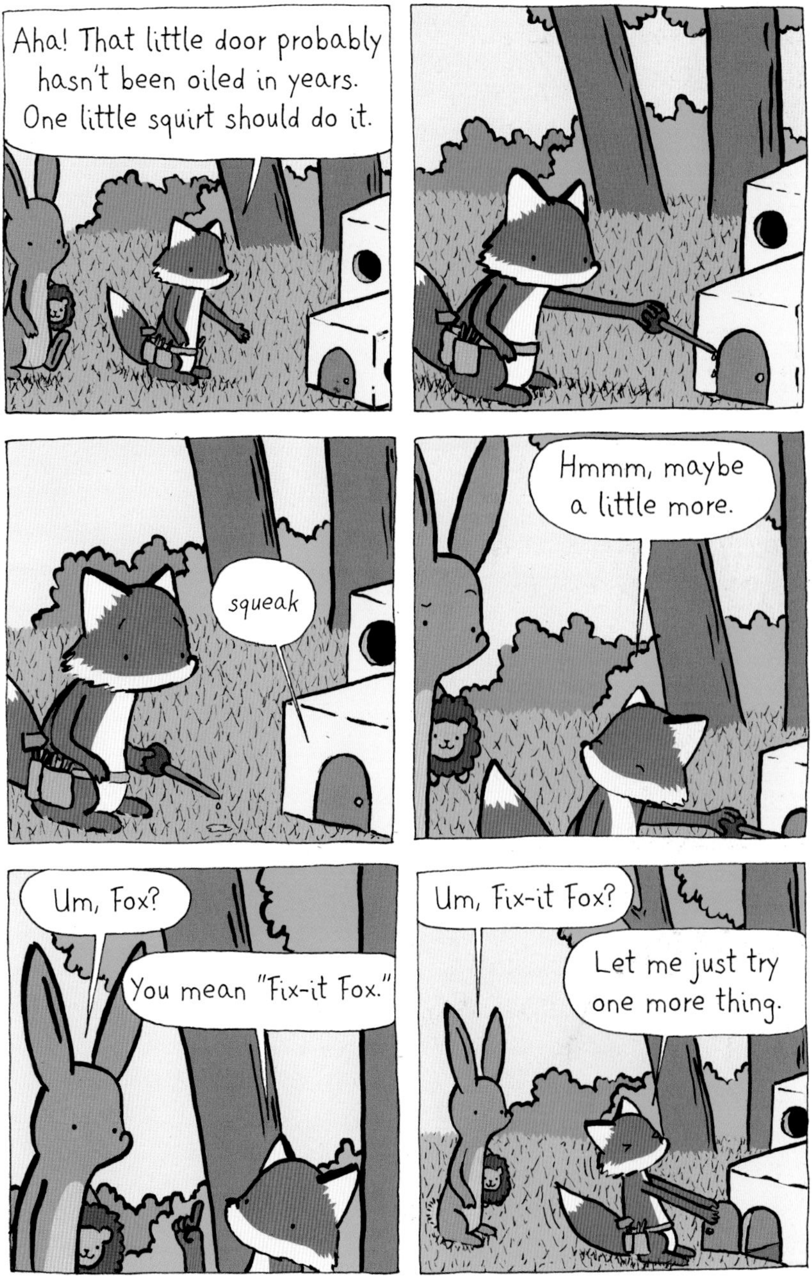
Aha! That little door probably hasn't been oiled in years. One little squirt should do it.
squeak
Hmmm, maybe a little more.
Um, Fox?
You mean "Fix-it Fox."
Um, Fix-it Fox?
Let me just try one more thing.

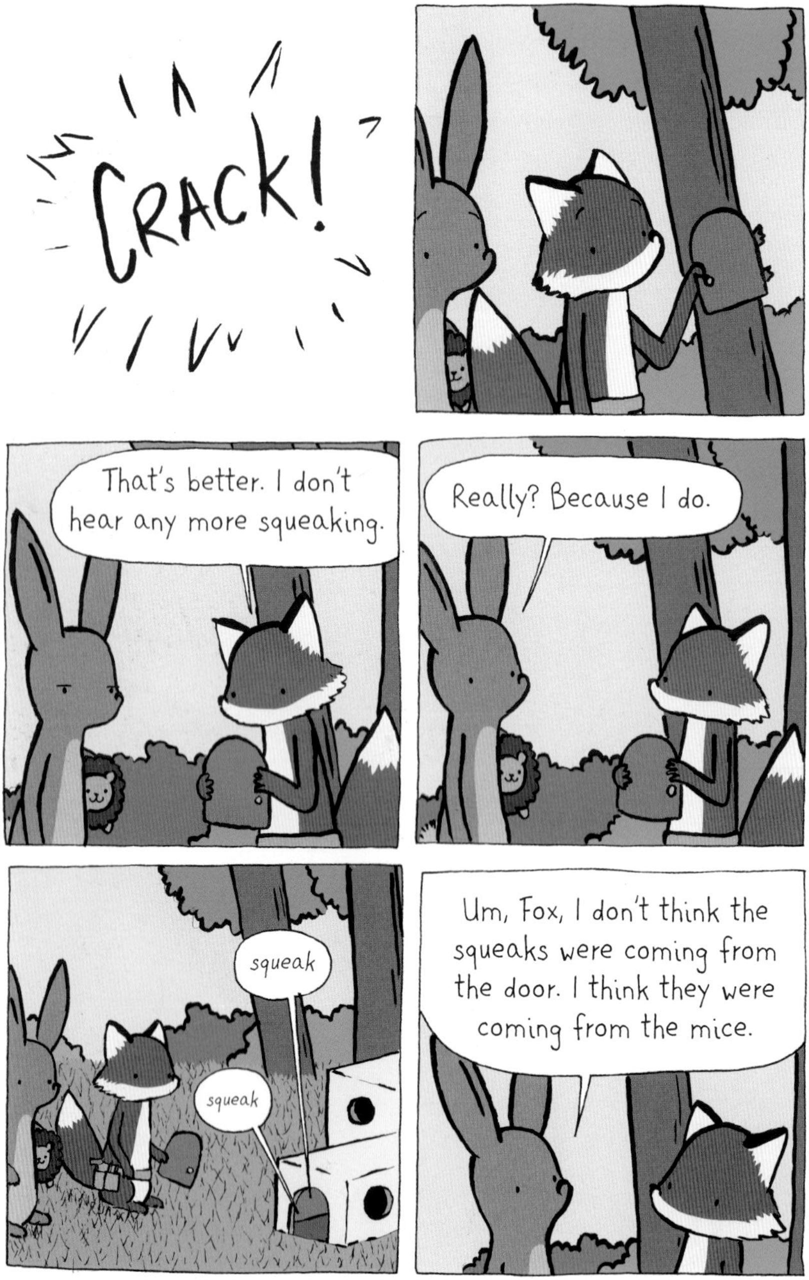
CRACK!
That's better. I don't hear any more squeaking.
Really? Because I do.
squeak
squeak
Um, Fox, I don't think the squeaks were coming from the door. I think they were coming from the mice.

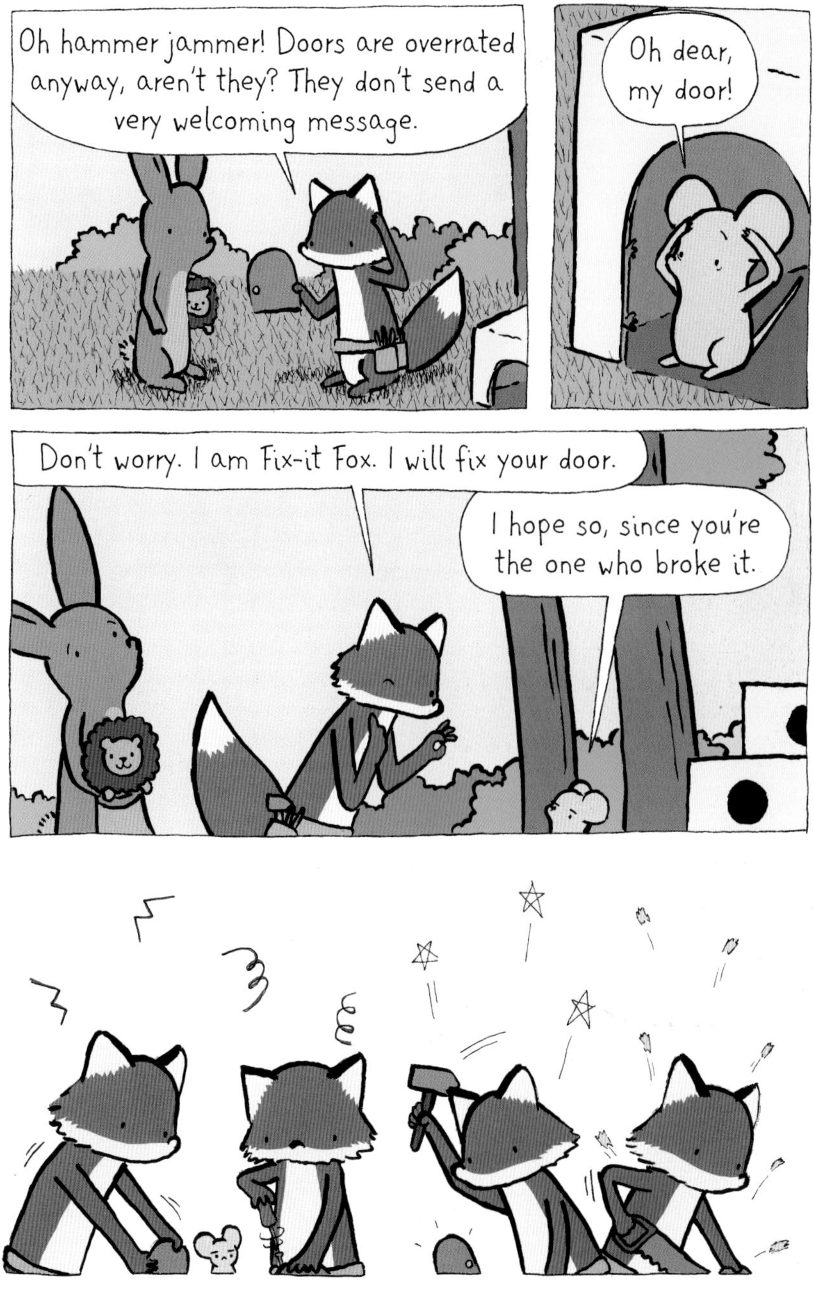
Oh hammer jammer! Doors are overrated anyway, aren't they? They don't send a very welcoming message.
Oh dear, my door!
Don't worry. I am Fix-it Fox. I will fix your door.
I hope so, since you're the one who broke it.

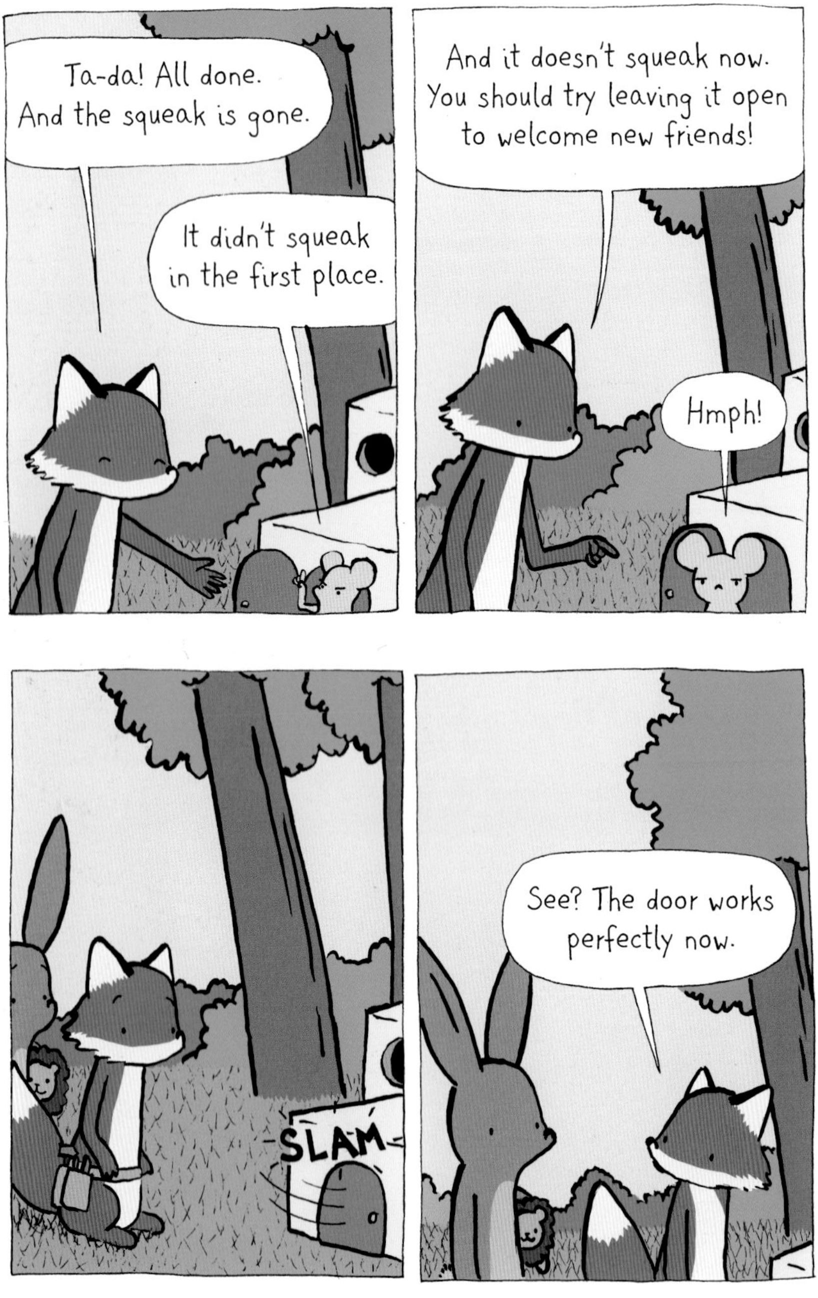
Ta-da! All done.
And the squeak is gone.
It didn't squeak
in the first place.
And it doesn't squeak now.
You should try leaving it open
to welcome new friends!
Hmph!
SLAM
See? The door works
perfectly now.

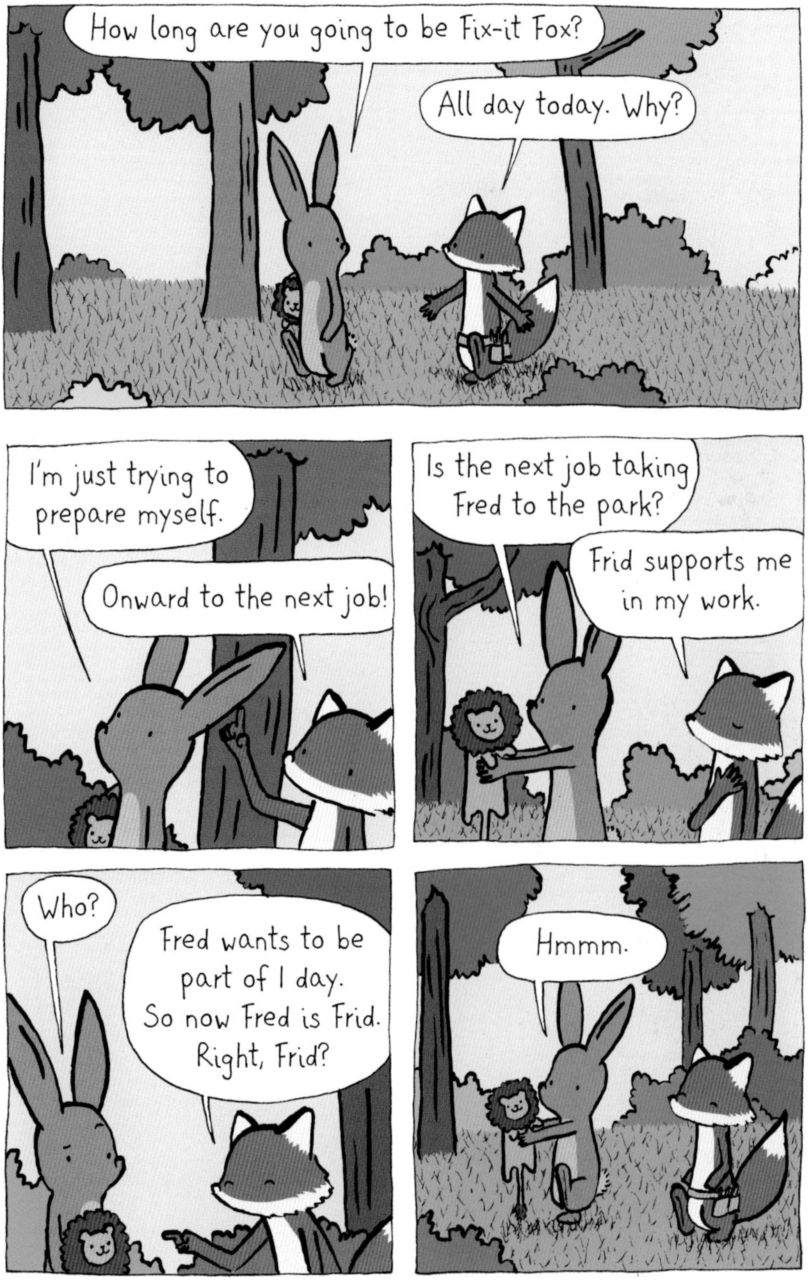
How long are you going to be Fix-it Fox?
All day today. Why?
I'm just trying to prepare myself.
Onward to the next job!
Is the next job taking Fred to the park?
Frid supports me in my work.
Who?
Fred wants to be part of 1 day. So now Fred is Frid. Right, Frid?
Hmmm.

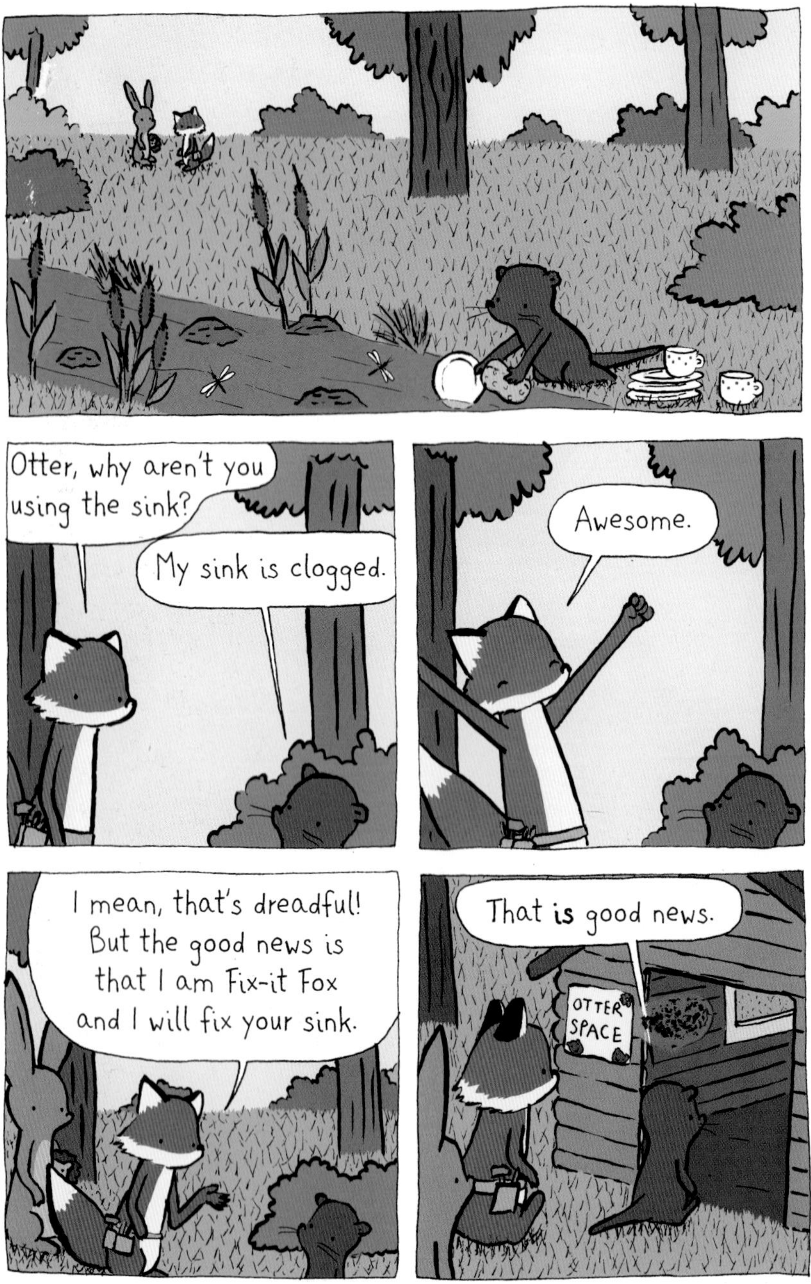
Otter, why aren't you using the sink?
My sink is clogged.
Awesome.
I mean, that's dreadful! But the good news is that I am Fix-it Fox and I will fix your sink.
That is good news.
OTTER SPACE

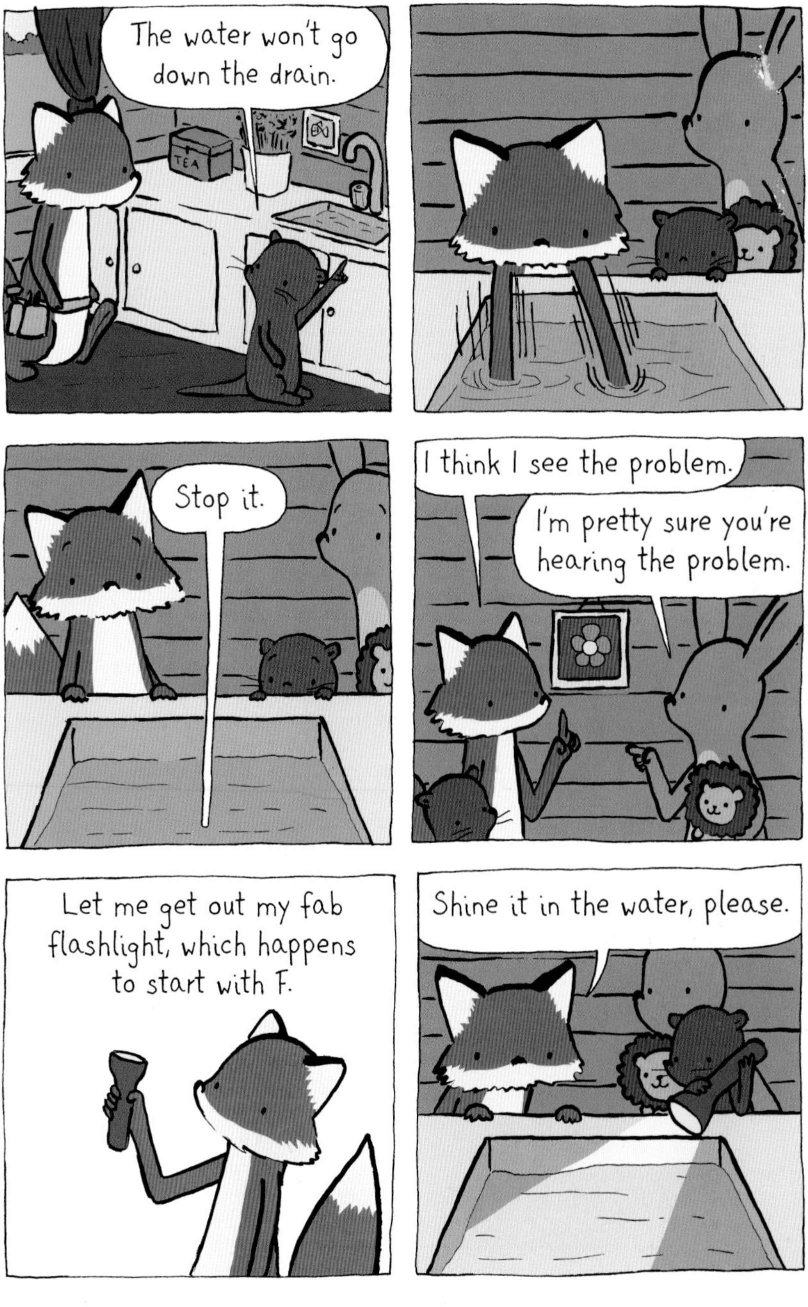
The water won't go down the drain.
Stop it.
I think I see the problem.
I'm pretty sure you're hearing the problem.
Let me get out my fab flashlight, which happens to start with F.
Shine it in the water, please.

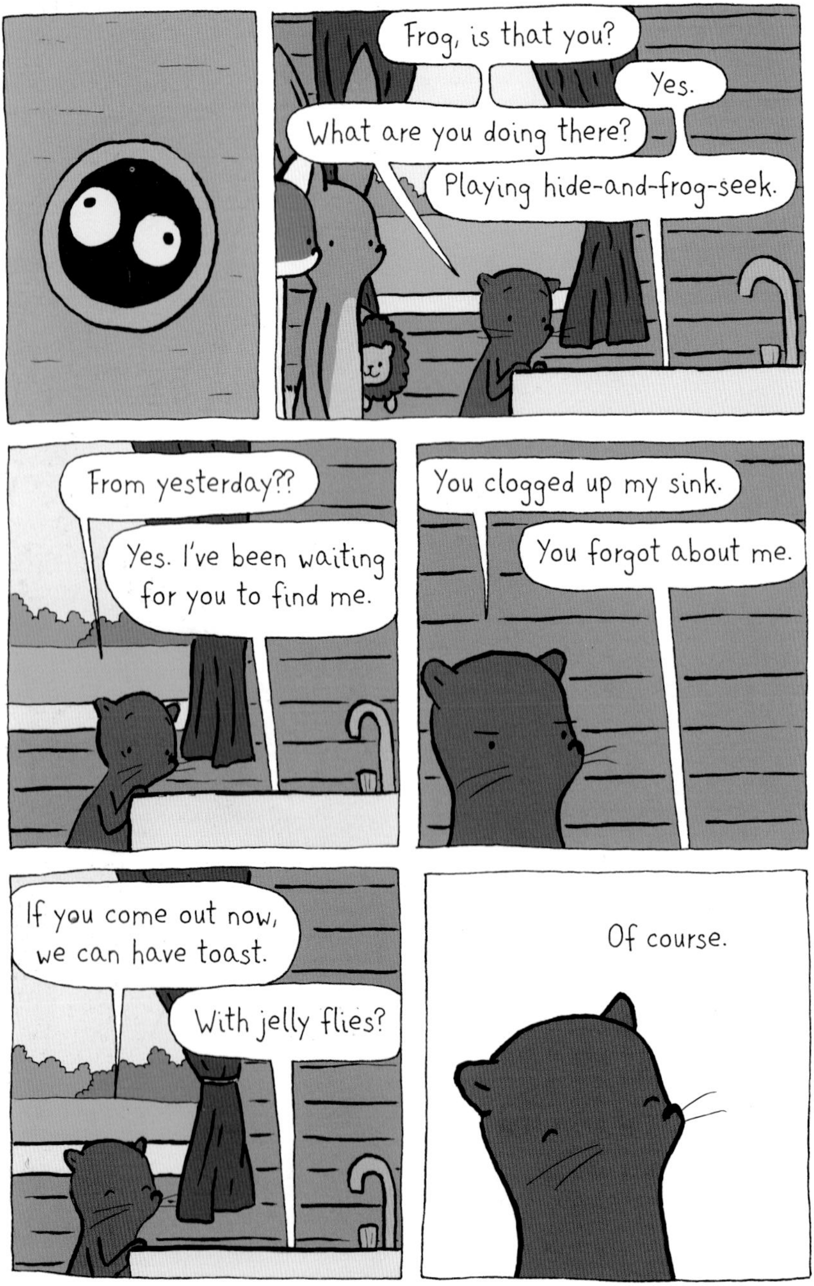
Frog, is that you?
Yes.
What are you doing there?
Playing hide-and-frog-seek.
From yesterday??
Yes. I've been waiting for you to find me.
You clogged up my sink.
You forgot about me.
If you come out now, we can have toast.
With jelly flies?
Of course.

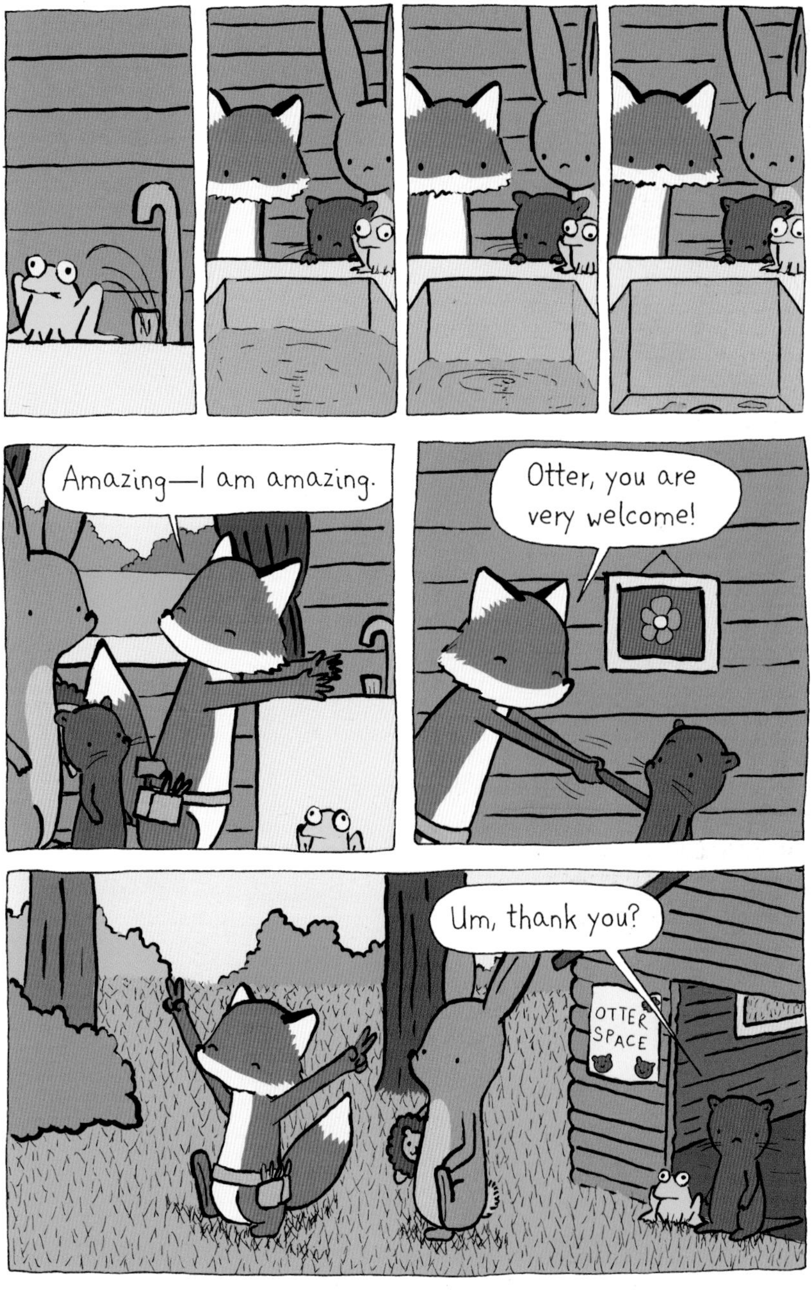
Amazing—I am amazing.
Otter, you are very welcome!
Um, thank you?
OTTER SPACE

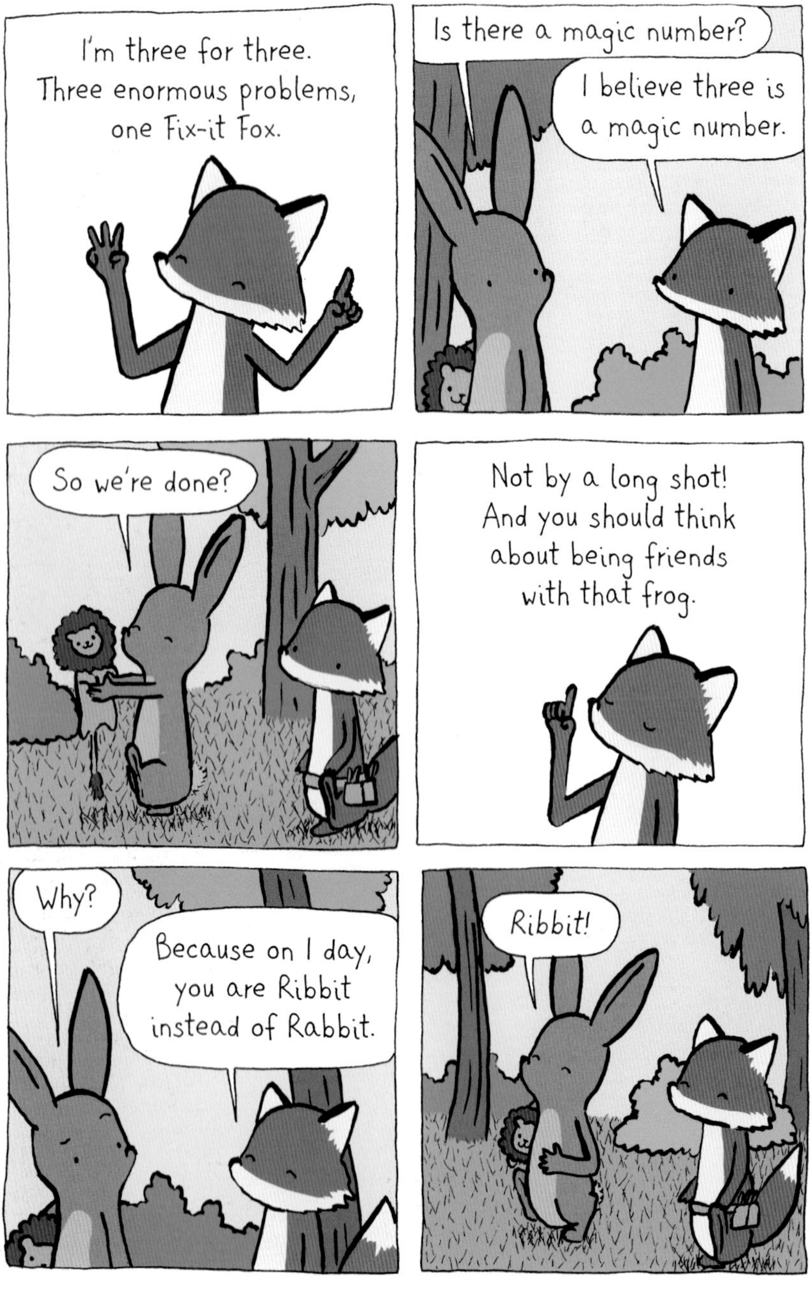
I'm three for three. Three enormous problems, one Fix-it Fox.
Is there a magic number?
I believe three is a magic number.
So we're done?
Not by a long shot! And you should think about being friends with that frog.
Why?
Because on 1 day, you are Ribbit instead of Rabbit.
Ribbit!

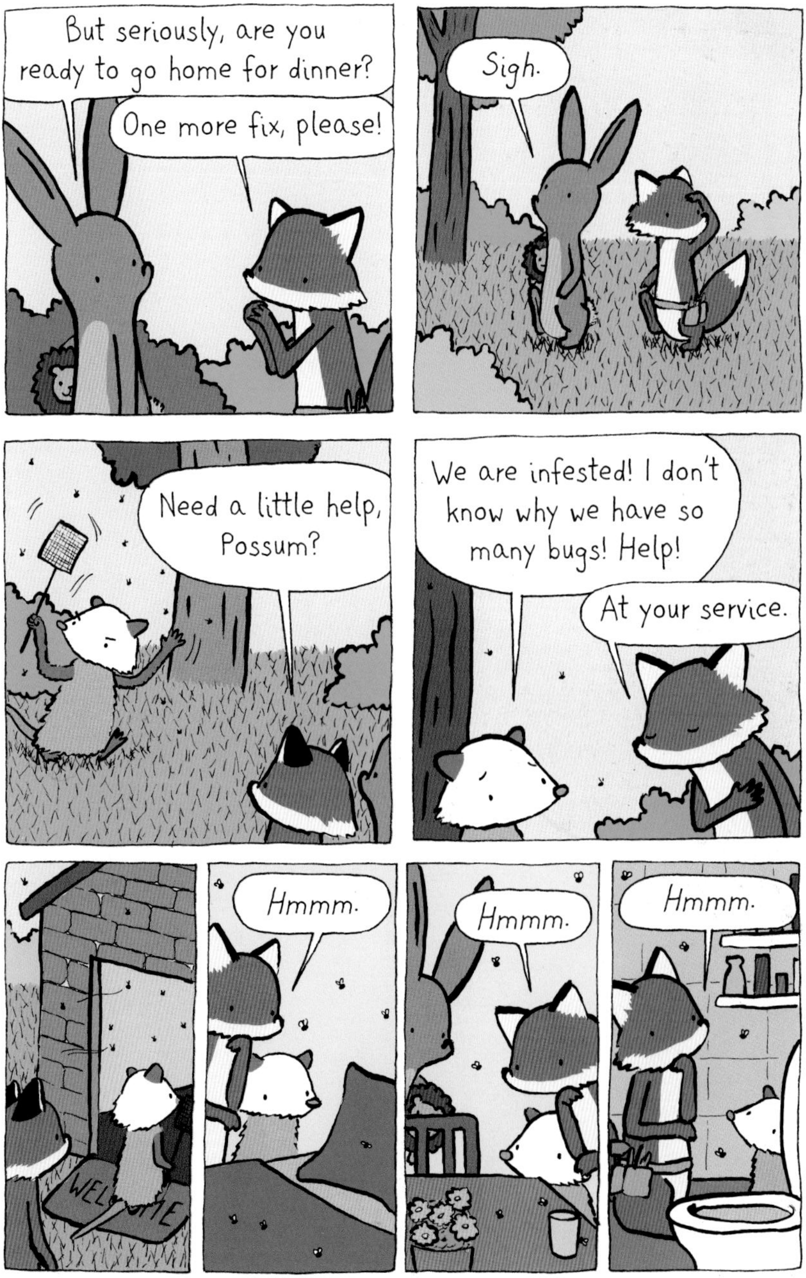
But seriously, are you ready to go home for dinner?
One more fix, please!
Sigh.
Need a little help, Possum?
We are infested! I don't know why we have so many bugs! Help!
At your service.
WELCOME
Hmmm.
Hmmm.
Hmmm.

I see the problem.
Oh, thank goodness! I need to feed the joeys dinner.
WELCOME
There! That should do the trick. Now that they're not welcome, all the bugs will leave.
Oh!
Oh dear.
Wait! I have another idea.
COOKIES

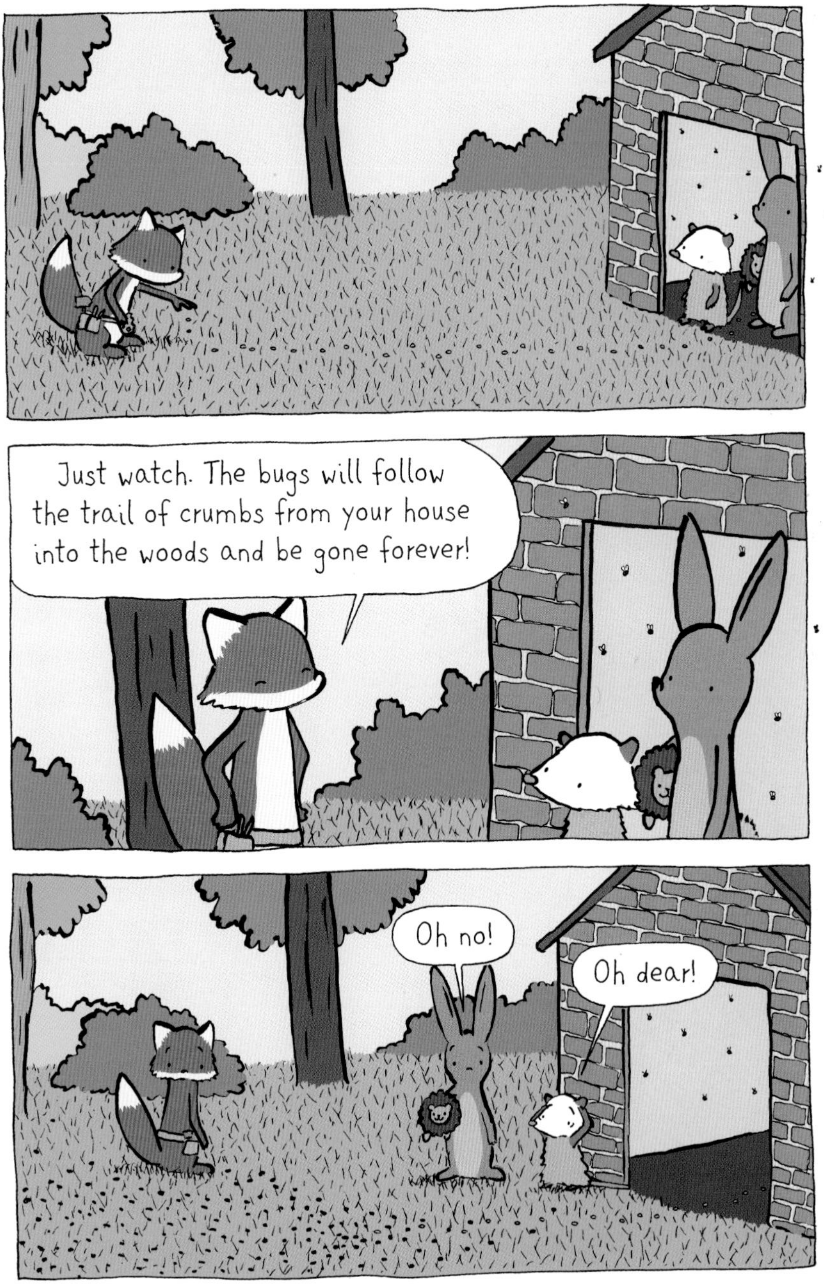
Just watch. The bugs will follow the trail of crumbs from your house into the woods and be gone forever!
Oh no!
Oh dear!

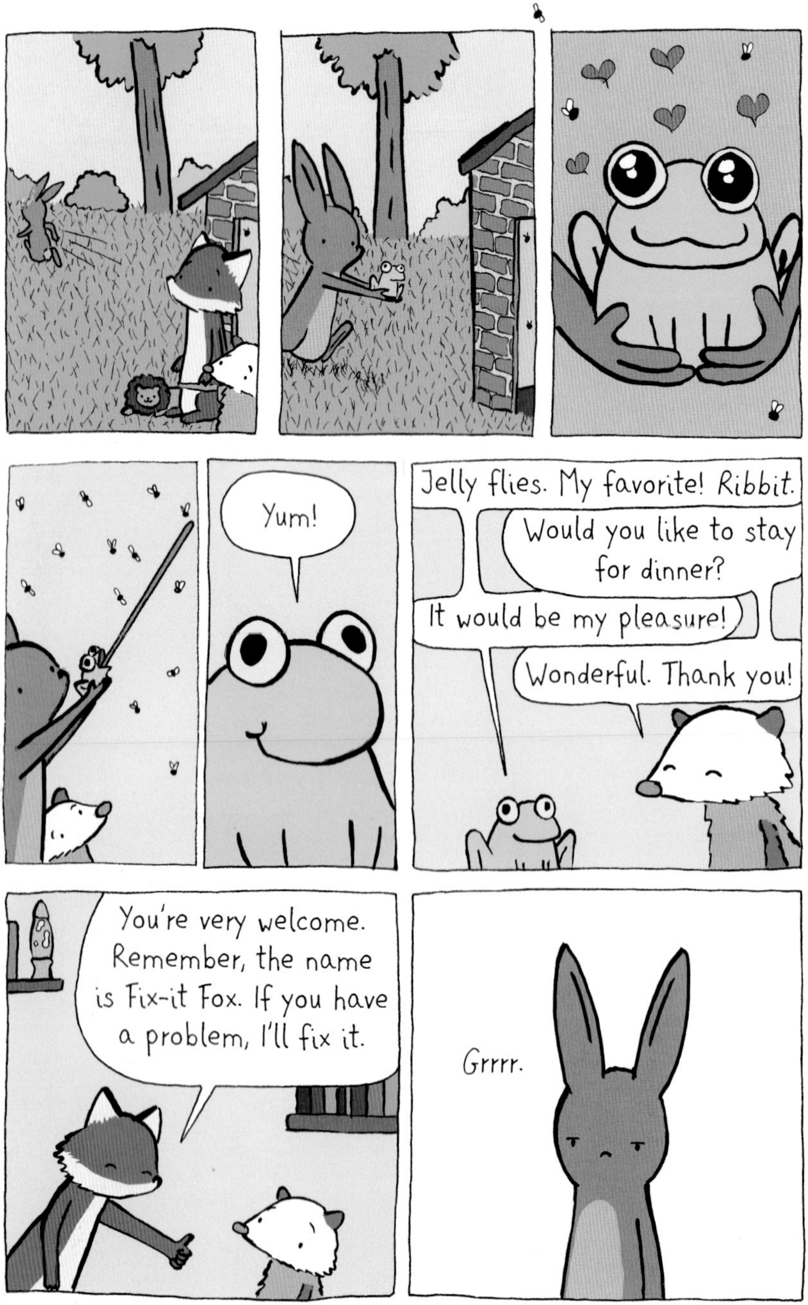
Yum!
Jelly flies. My favorite! *Ribbit.*
Would you like to stay for dinner?
It would be my pleasure!
Wonderful. Thank you!
You're very welcome. Remember, the name is Fix-it Fox. If you have a problem, I'll fix it.
Grrrr.

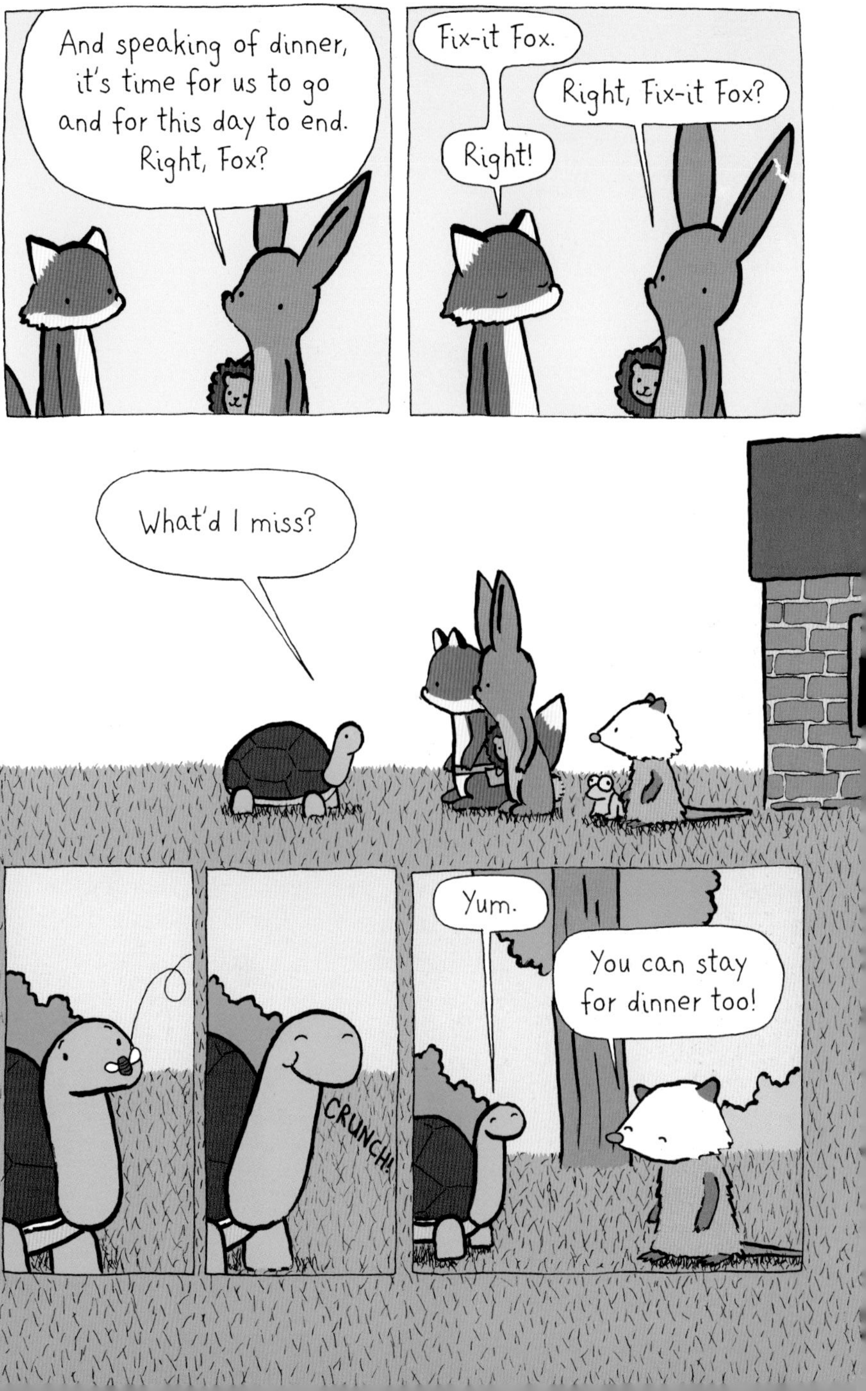
And speaking of dinner, it's time for us to go and for this day to end. Right, Fox?
Fix-it Fox.
Right!
Right, Fix-it Fox?
What'd I miss?
CRUNCH!
Yum.
You can stay for dinner too!

STORY TWO

PARTY, PIZZA & PLANS

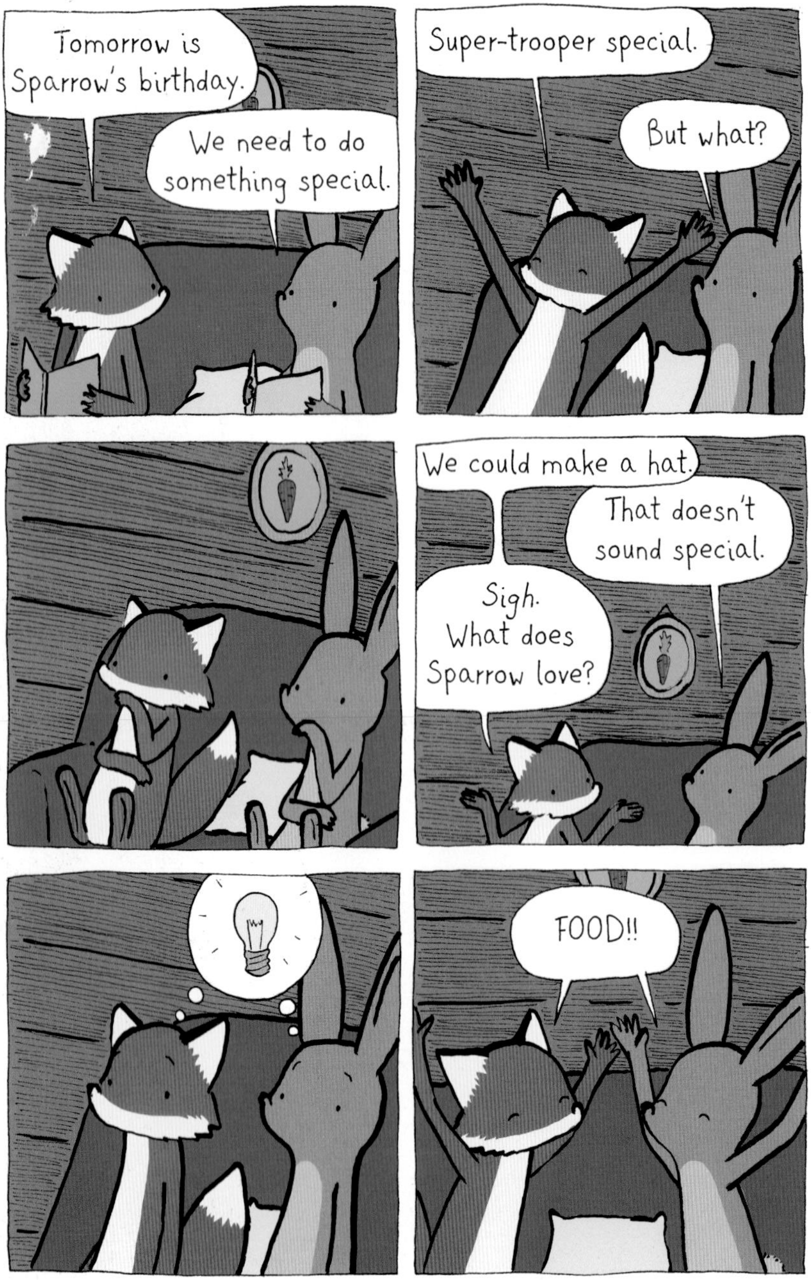
Tomorrow is Sparrow's birthday.
We need to do something special.
Super-trooper special.
But what?
We could make a hat.
That doesn't sound special.
Sigh. What does Sparrow love?
FOOD!!

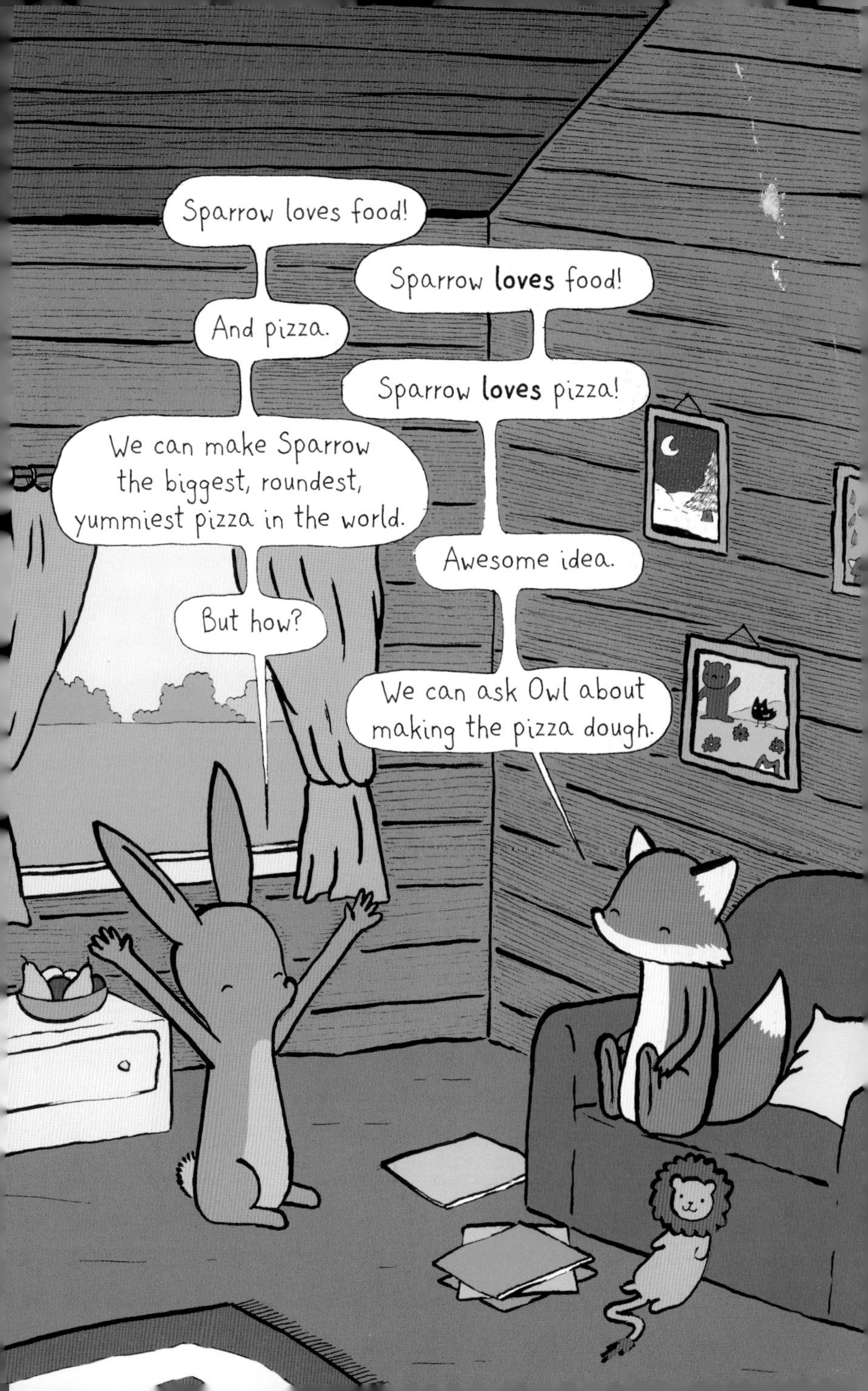
Sparrow loves food!
Sparrow **loves** food!
And pizza.
Sparrow **loves** pizza!
We can make Sparrow the biggest, roundest, yummiest pizza in the world.
Awesome idea.
But how?
We can ask Owl about making the pizza dough.

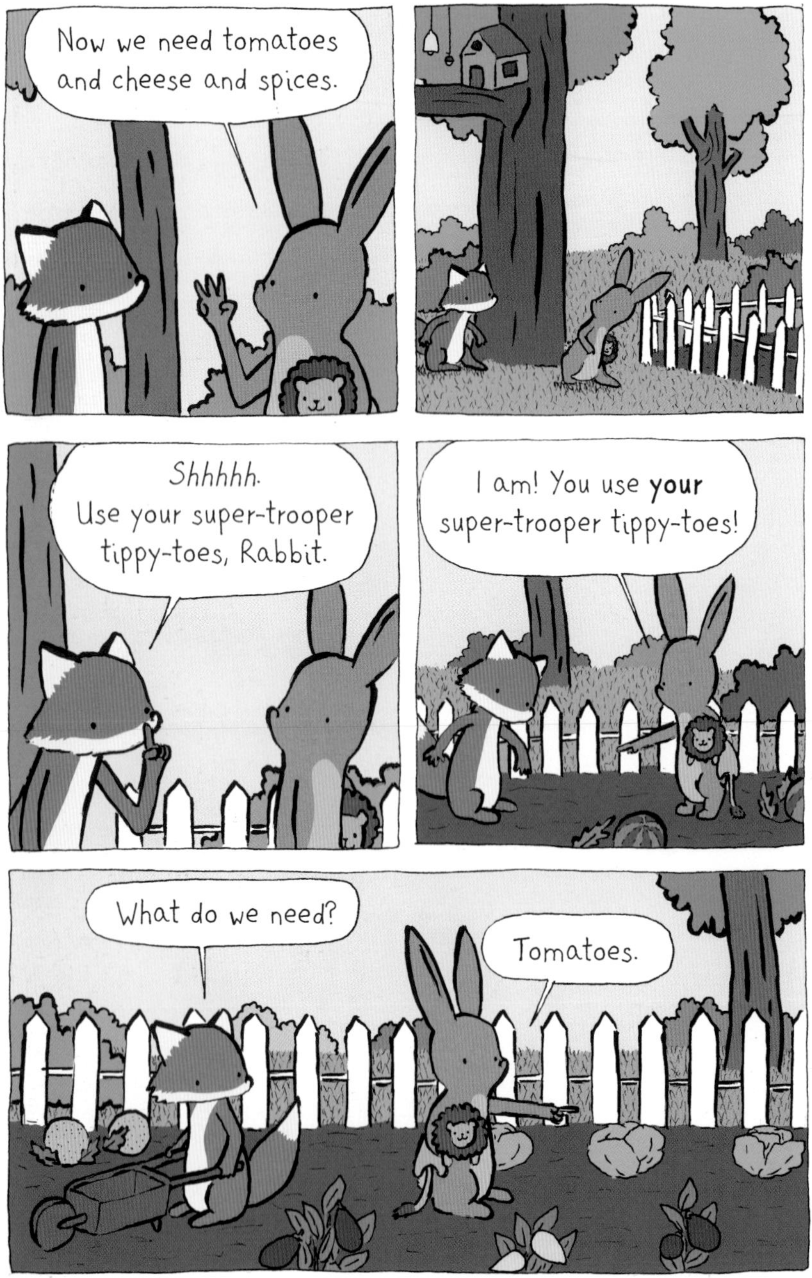
Now we need tomatoes and cheese and spices.
Shhhhh.
Use your super-trooper tippy-toes, Rabbit.
I am! You use **your** super-trooper tippy-toes!
What do we need?
Tomatoes.

32

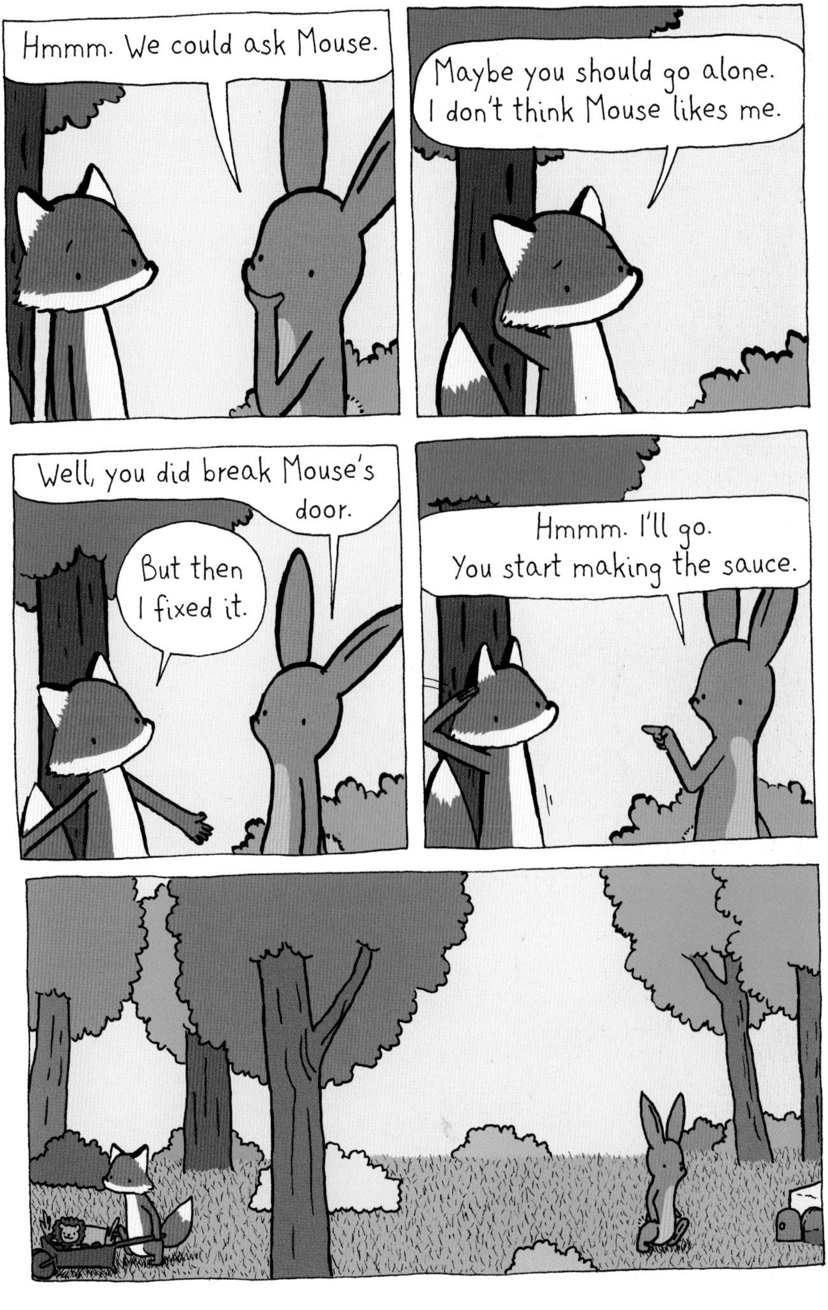
Hmmm. We could ask Mouse.
Maybe you should go alone. I don't think Mouse likes me.
Well, you did break Mouse's door.
But then I fixed it.
Hmmm. I'll go. You start making the sauce.

35

STORY THREE

DARING DRAGON DAYS

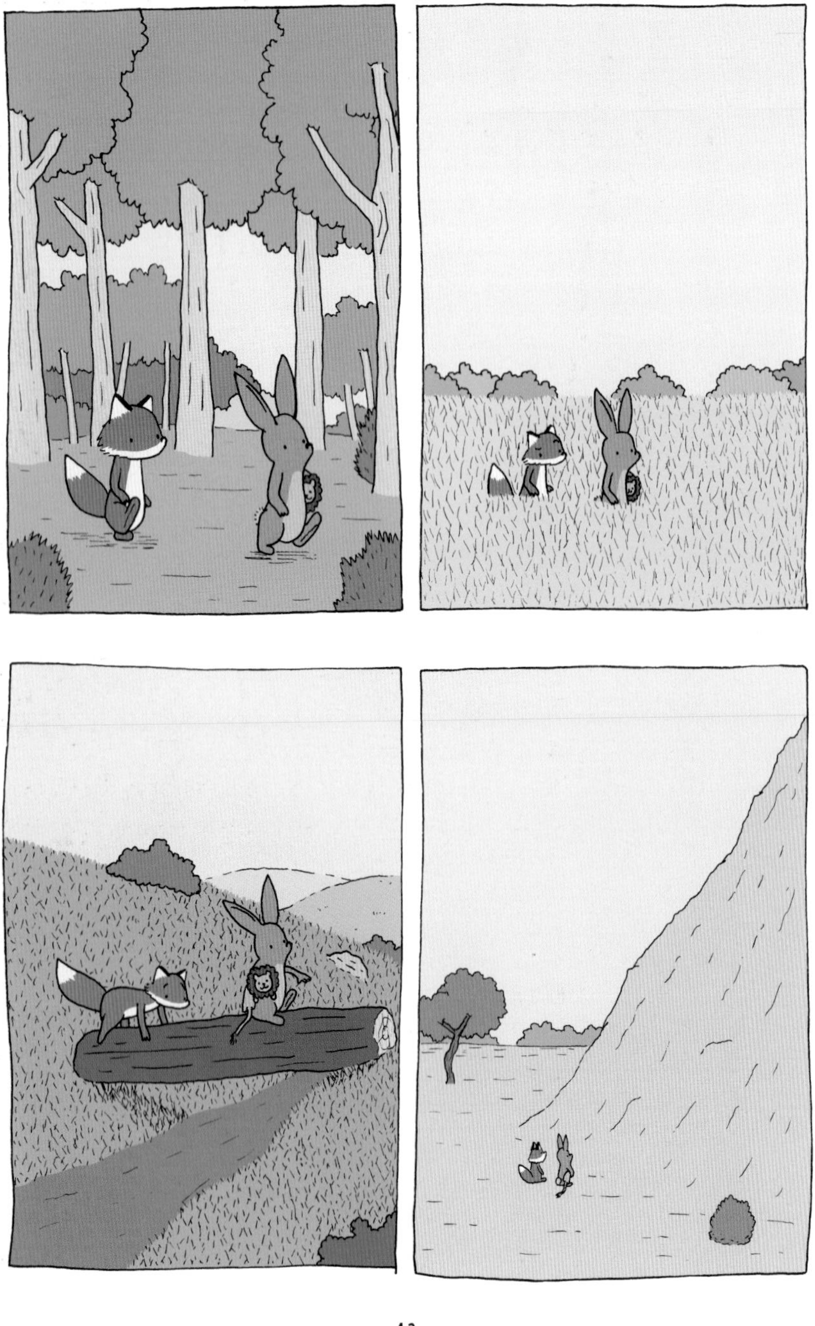

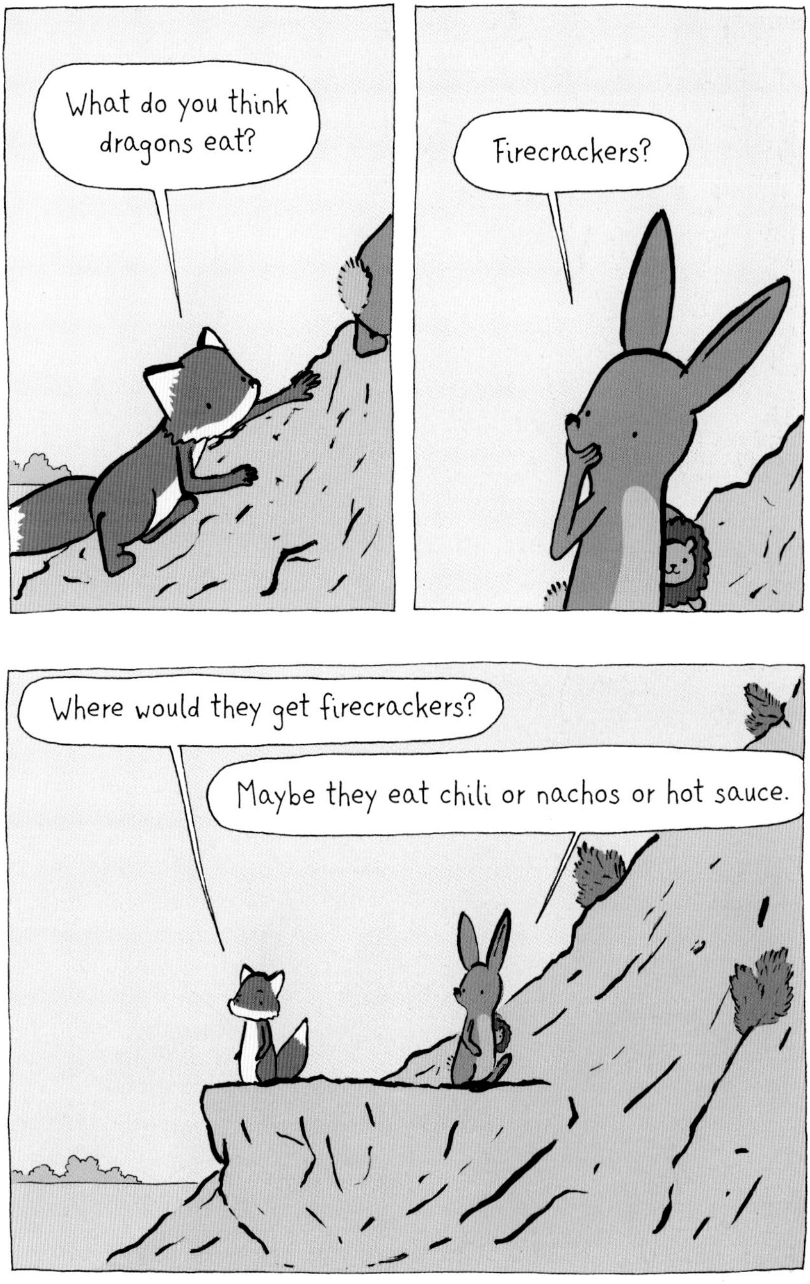
What do you think dragons eat?
Firecrackers?
Where would they get firecrackers?
Maybe they eat chili or nachos or hot sauce.

44

45

46

47

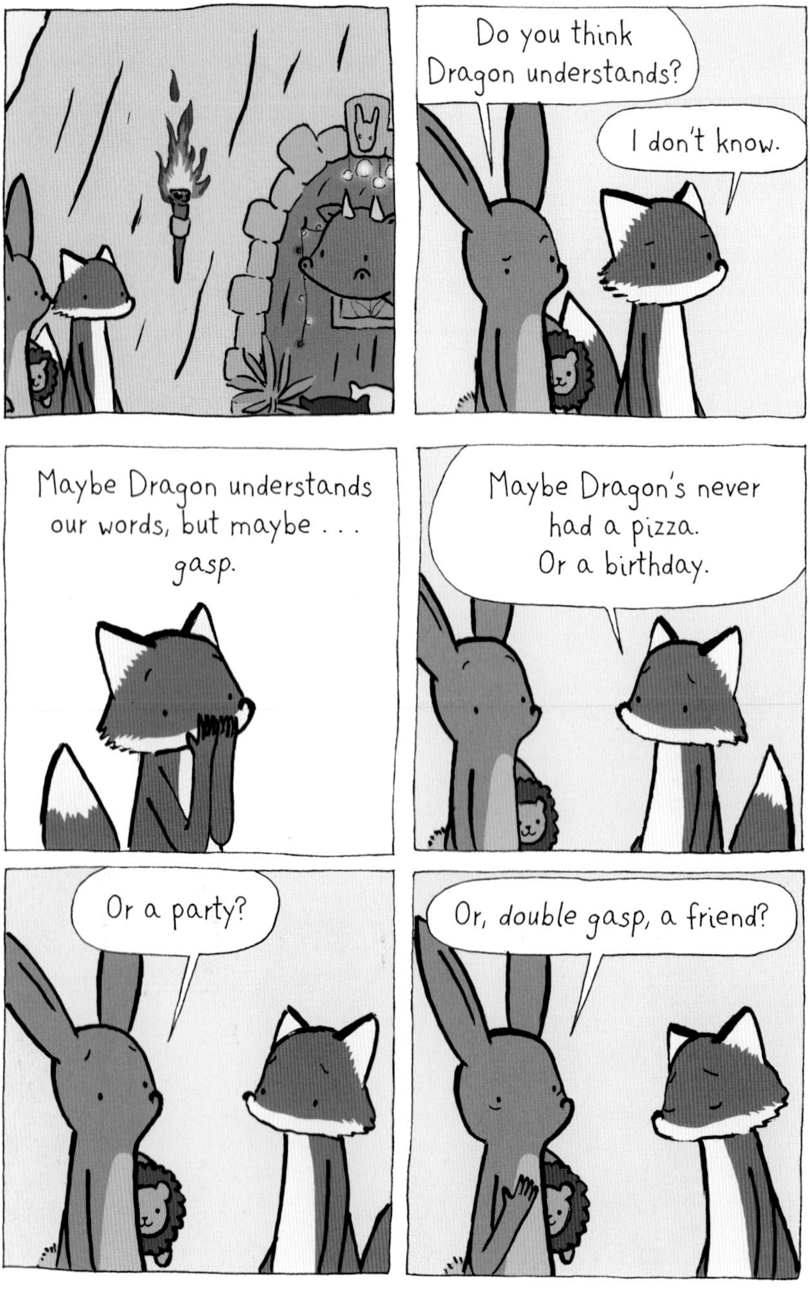
Do you think Dragon understands?
I don't know.
Maybe Dragon understands our words, but maybe . . . gasp.
Maybe Dragon's never had a pizza. Or a birthday.
Or a party?
Or, *double gasp*, a friend?

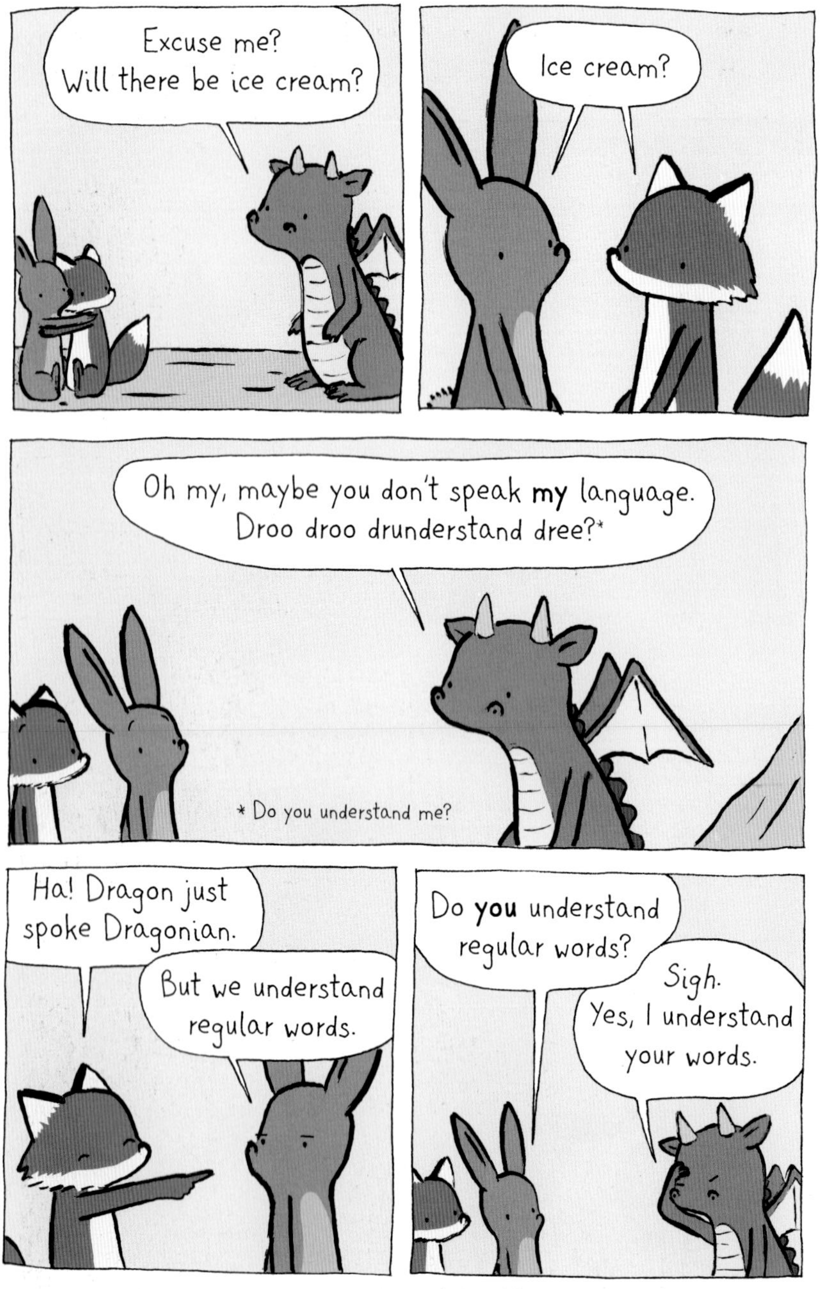
Excuse me?
Will there be ice cream?
Ice cream?
Oh my, maybe you don't speak **my** language. Droo droo drunderstand dree?*
* Do you understand me?
Ha! Dragon just spoke Dragonian.
But we understand regular words.
Do **you** understand regular words?
Sigh.
Yes, I understand your words.

It's everything else I don't understand. Why haven't I ever been invited to a party? Why is the sky blue? What does ice cream taste like? What does having a friend feel like?

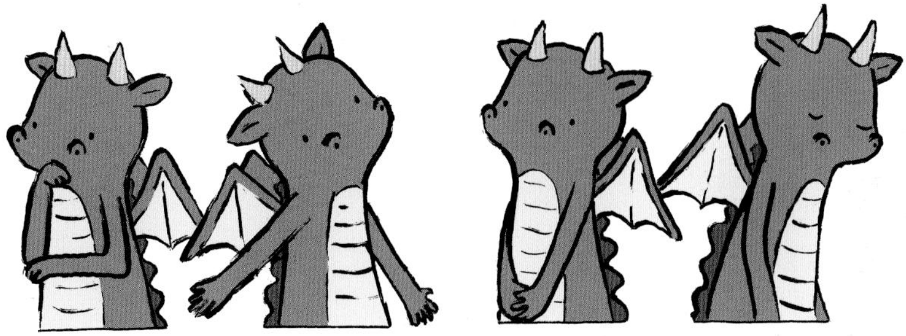

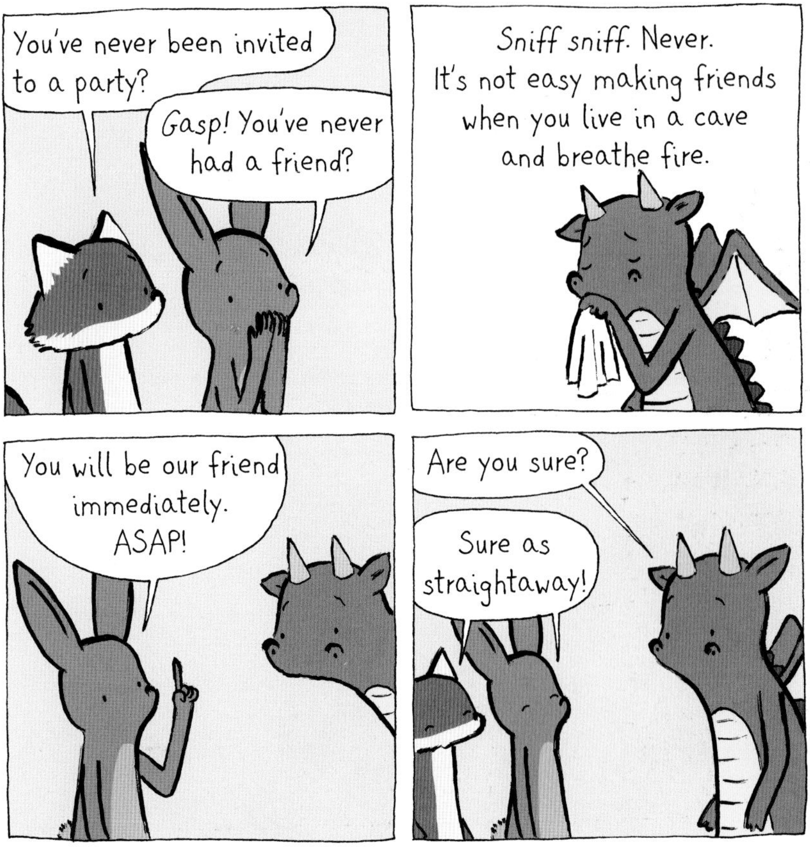
You've never been invited to a party?
Gasp! You've never had a friend?
Sniff sniff. Never.
It's not easy making friends when you live in a cave and breathe fire.
You will be our friend immediately. ASAP!
Are you sure?
Sure as straightaway!

BIRTHDAYS, BEST DAYS & BEST FRIENDS

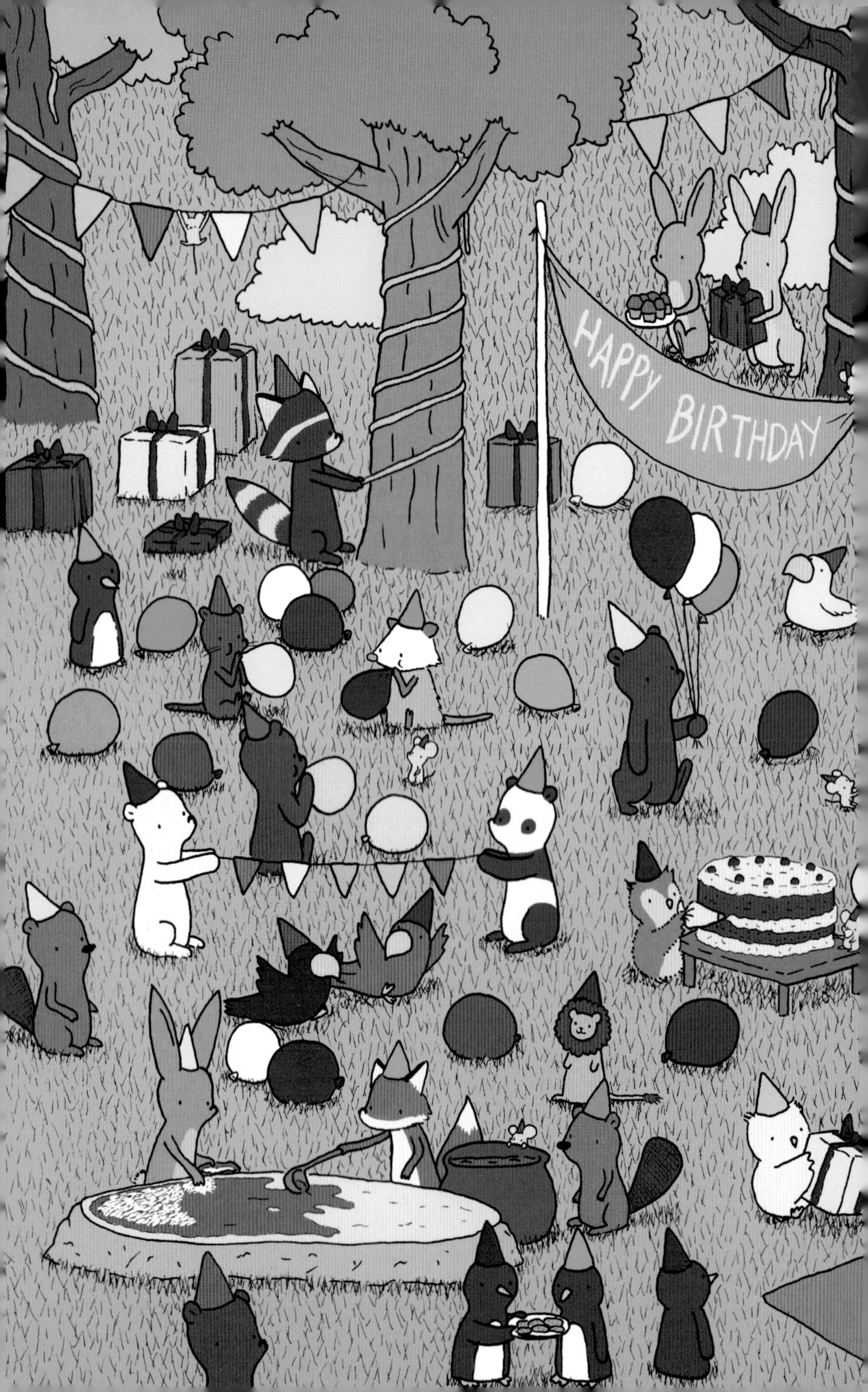
HAPPY BIRTHDAY

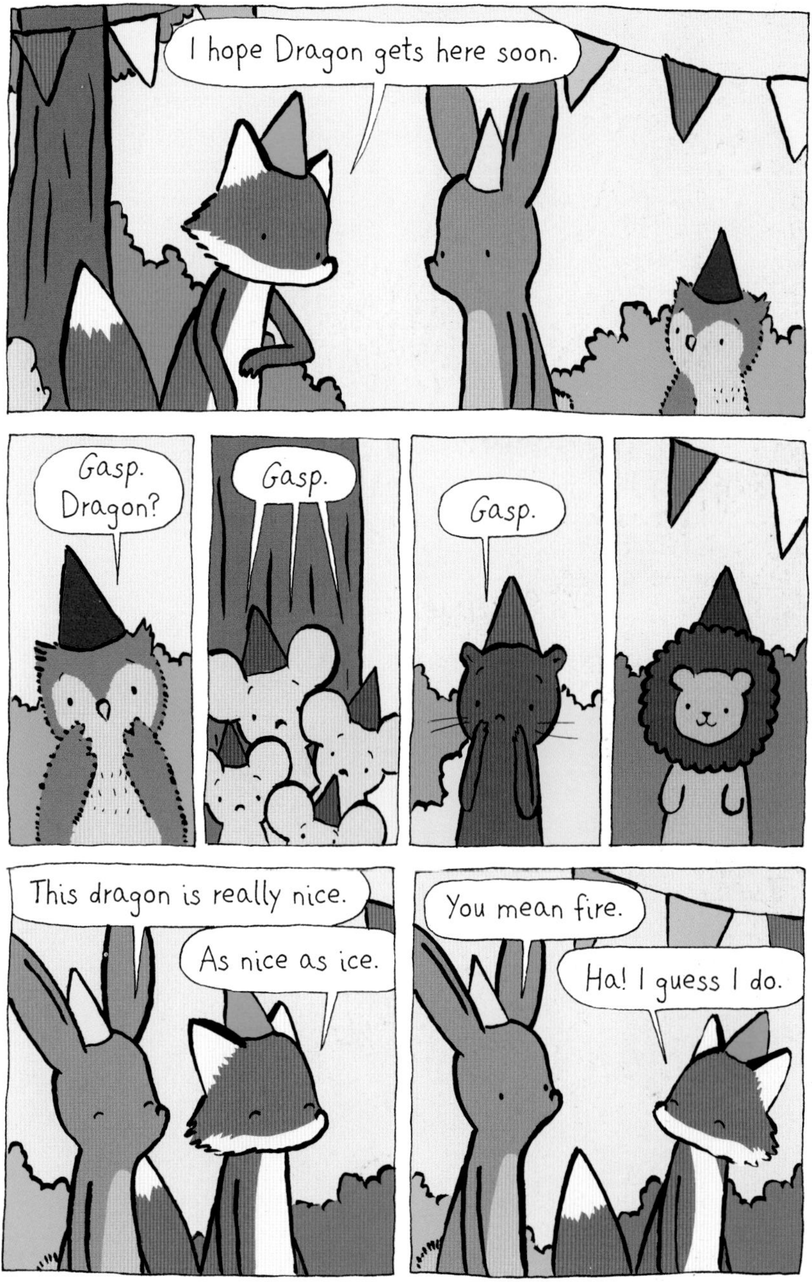
I hope Dragon gets here soon.
Gasp. Dragon?
Gasp.
Gasp.
This dragon is really nice.
As nice as ice.
You mean fire.
Ha! I guess I do.

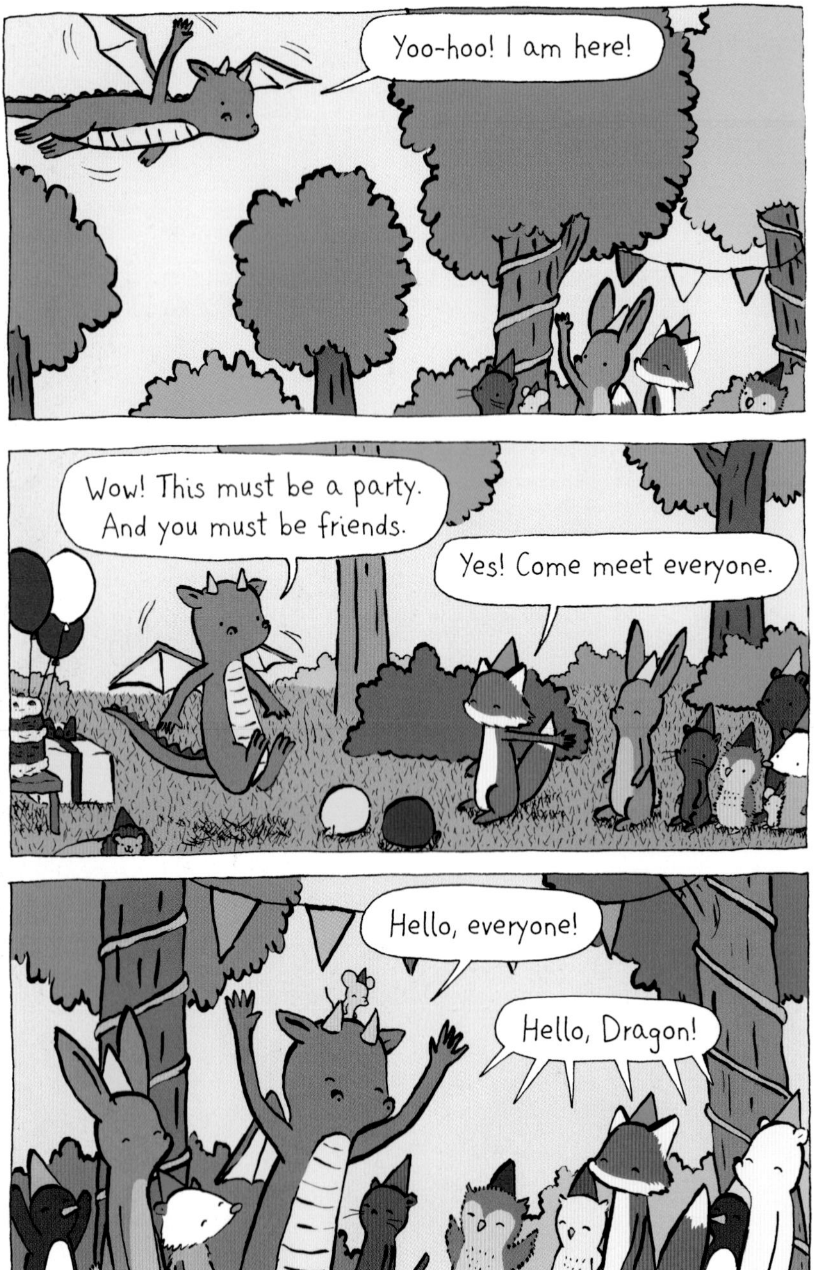
Yoo-hoo! I am here!
Wow! This must be a party. And you must be friends.
Yes! Come meet everyone.
Hello, everyone!
Hello, Dragon!

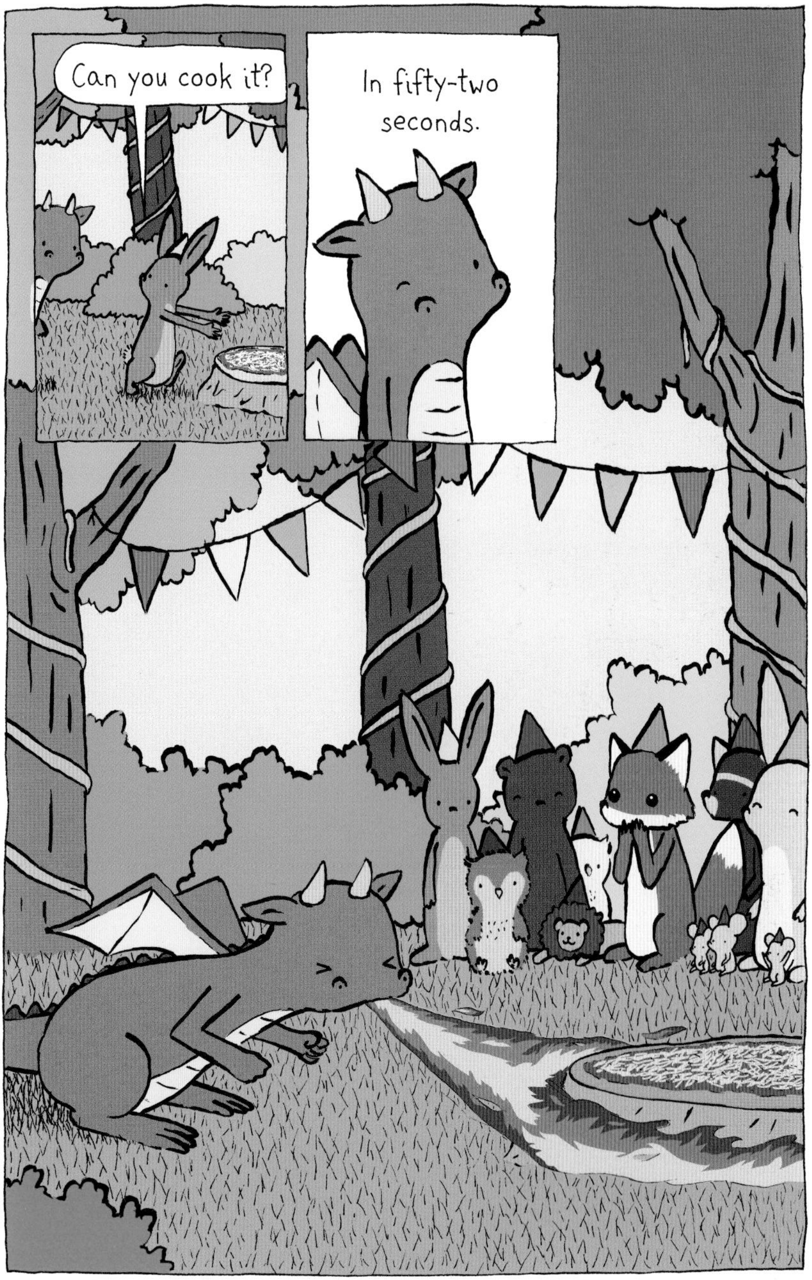
Can you cook it?
In fifty-two seconds.

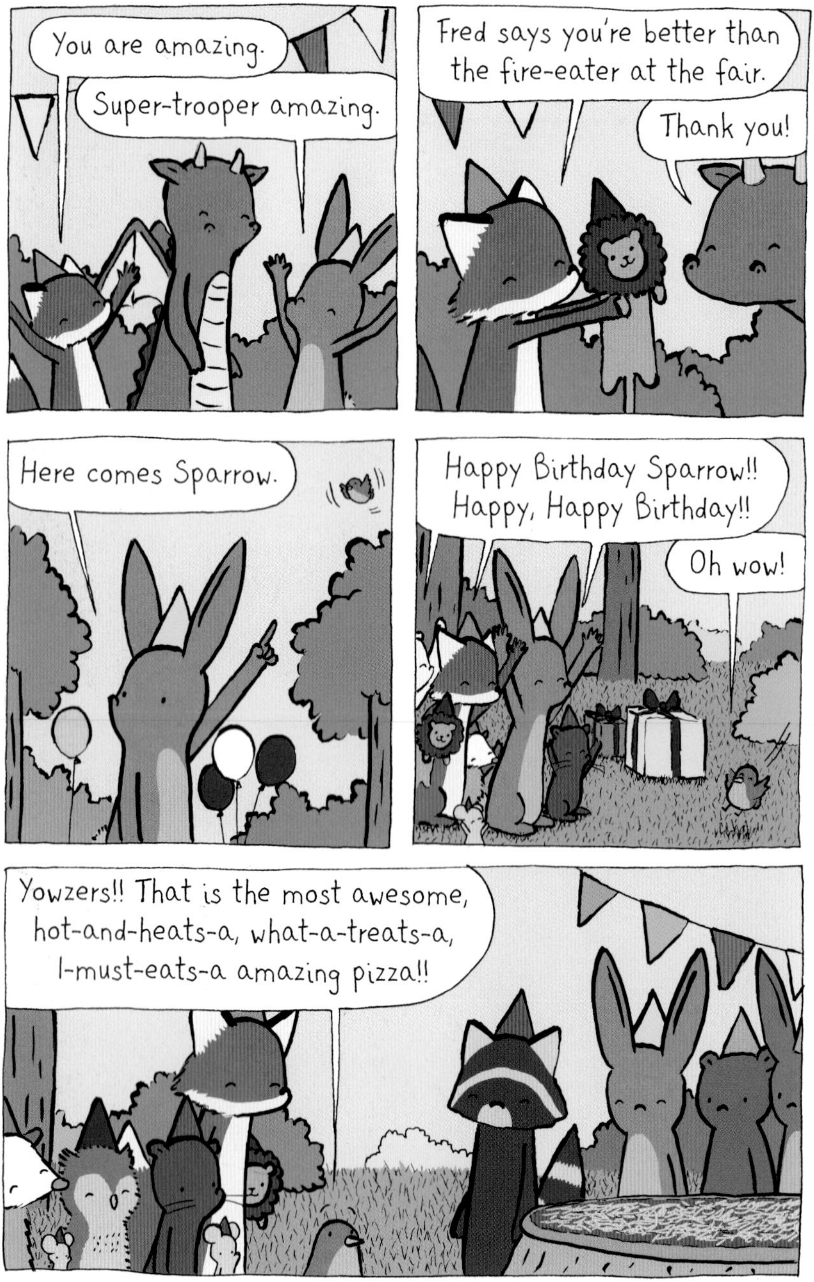
You are amazing.
Super-trooper amazing.
Fred says you're better than the fire-eater at the fair.
Thank you!
Here comes Sparrow.
Happy Birthday Sparrow!! Happy, Happy Birthday!!
Oh wow!
Yowzers!! That is the most awesome, hot-and-heats-a, what-a-treats-a, I-must-eats-a amazing pizza!!

61

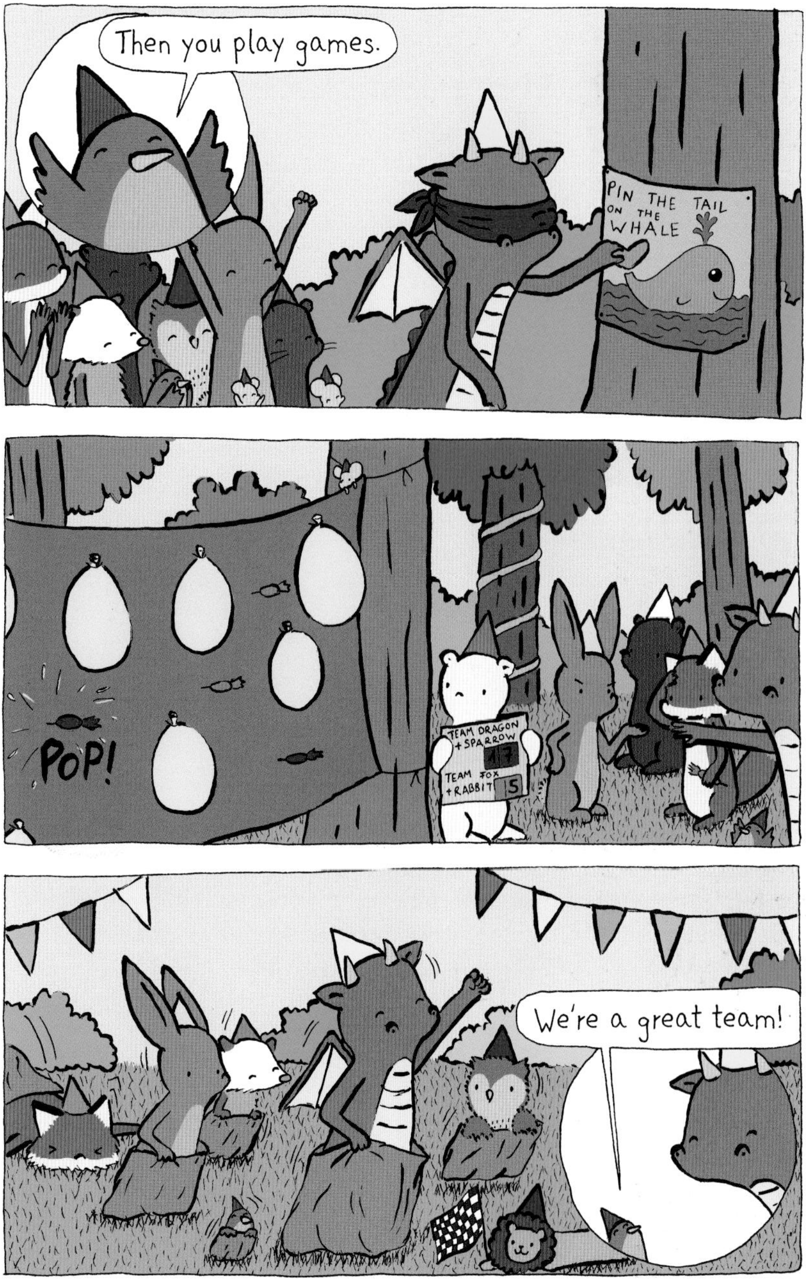
Then you play games.
PIN THE TAIL ON THE WHALE
POP!
TEAM DRAGON + SPARROW 17
TEAM FOX + RABBIT 5
We're a great team!

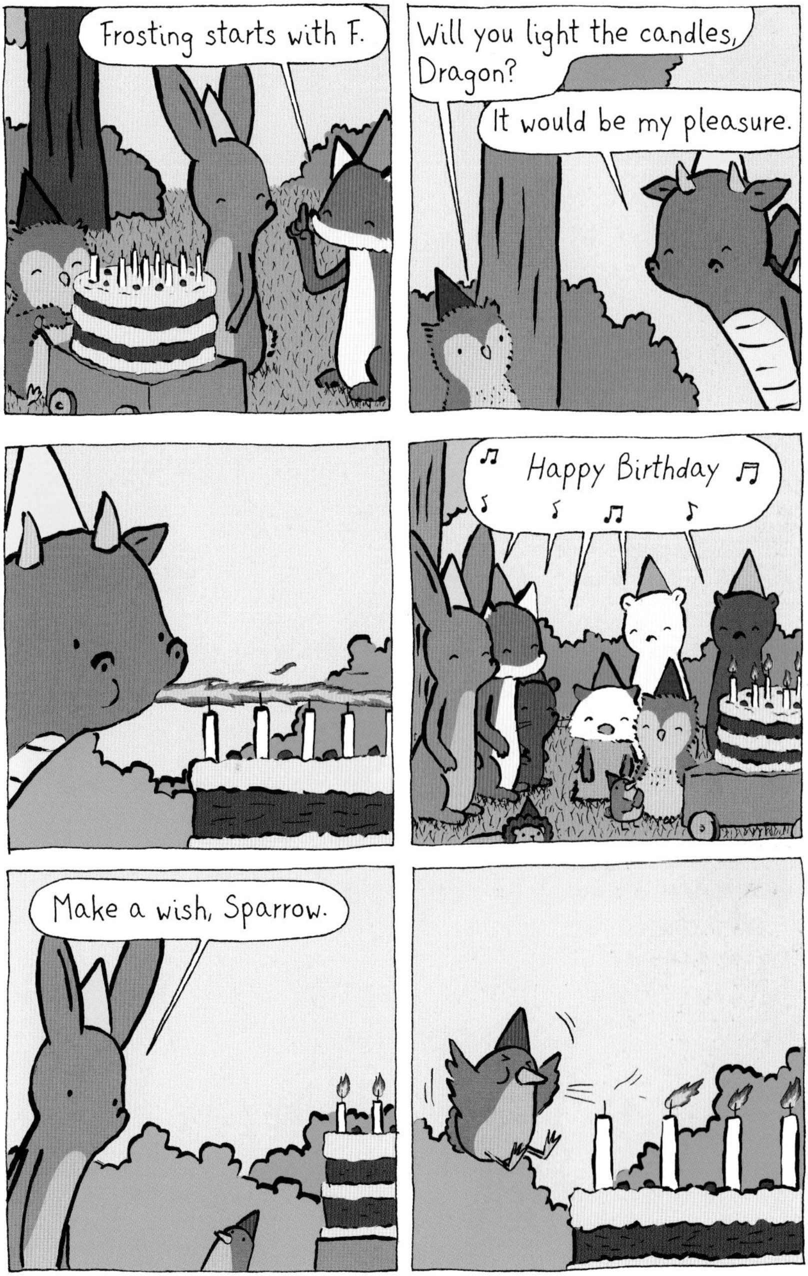

Frosting starts with F.
Will you light the candles, Dragon?
It would be my pleasure.
Happy Birthday
Make a wish, Sparrow.

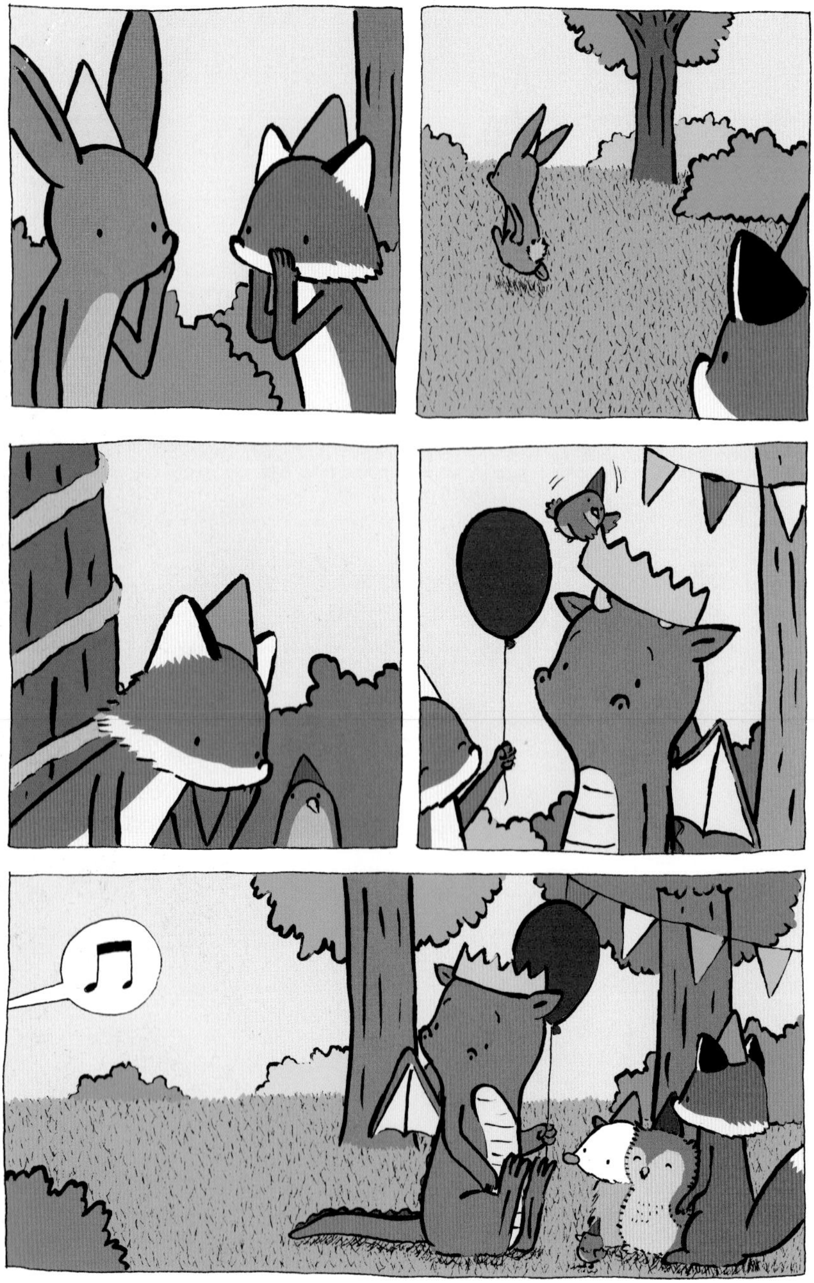

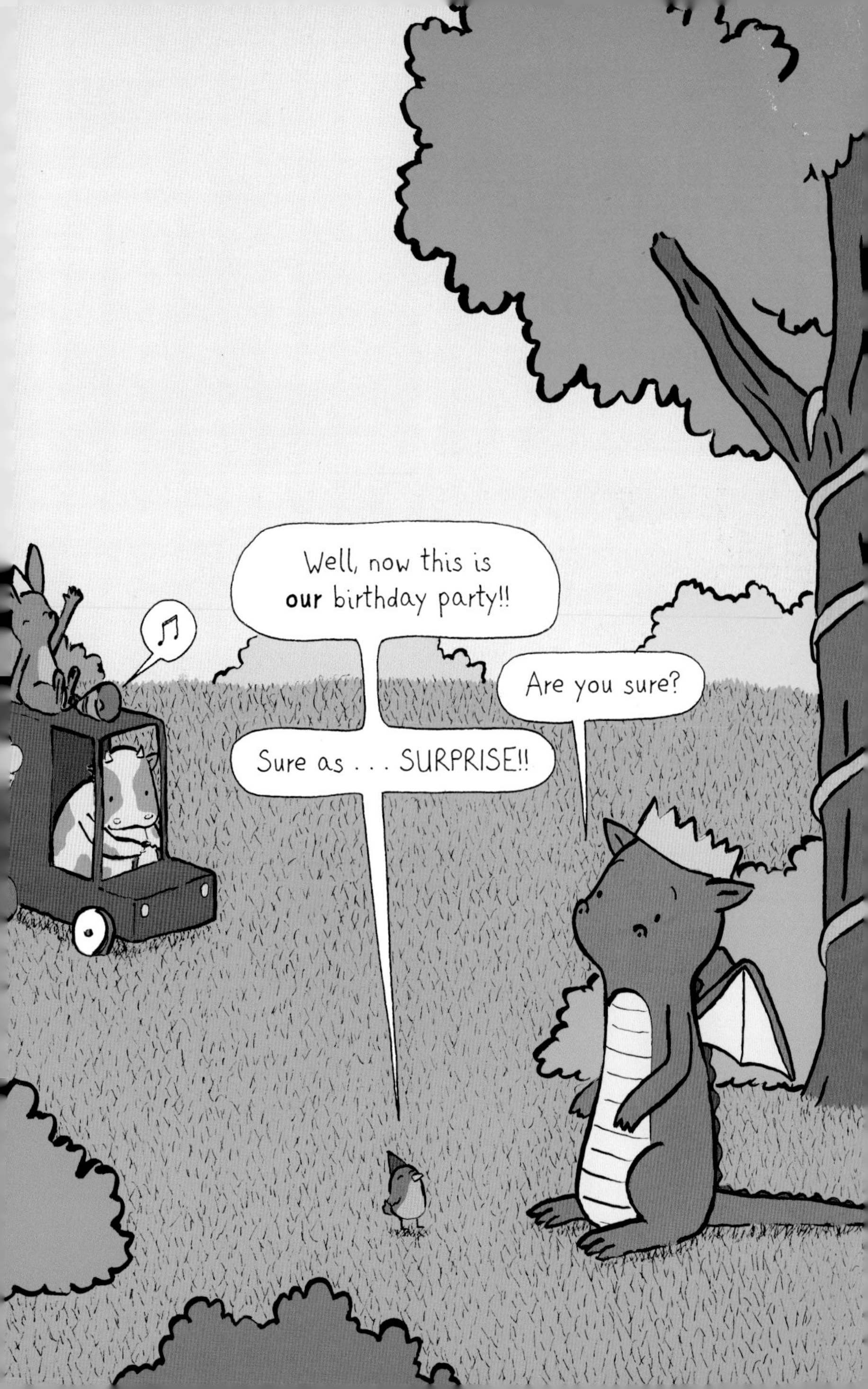
Well, now this is **our** birthday party!!
Are you sure?
Sure as . . . SURPRISE!!

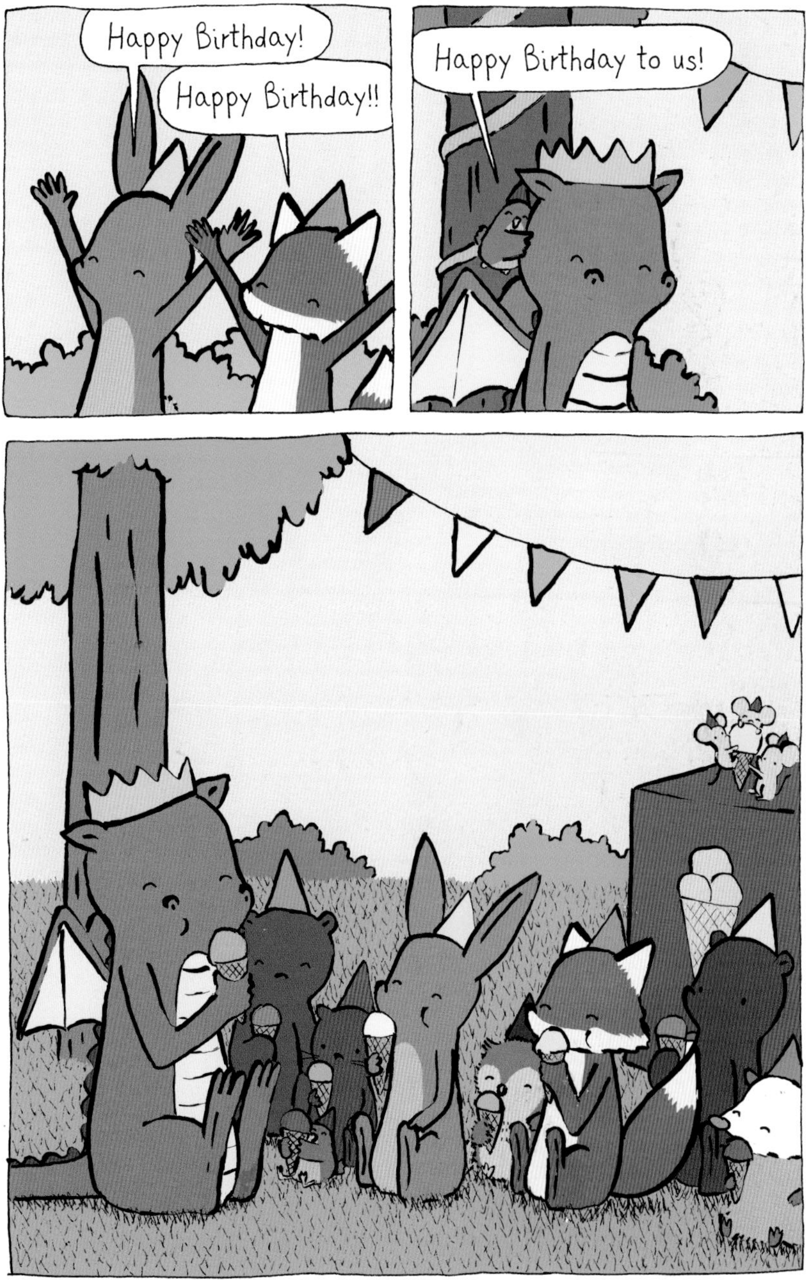
Happy Birthday!
Happy Birthday!!
Happy Birthday to us!

73

STORY FIVE

WONDER, WISH & WOW

81

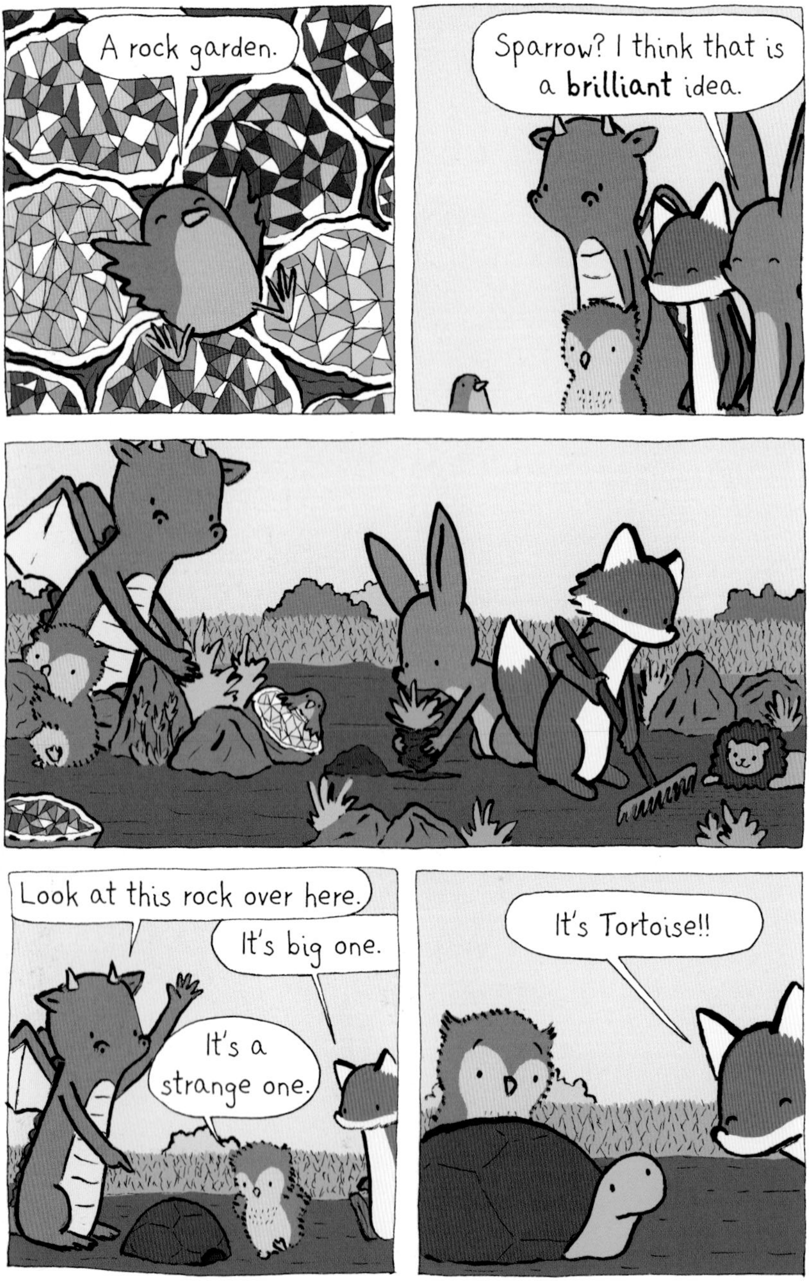
A rock garden.
Sparrow? I think that is a **brilliant** idea.
Look at this rock over here.
It's big one.
It's a strange one.
It's Tortoise!!

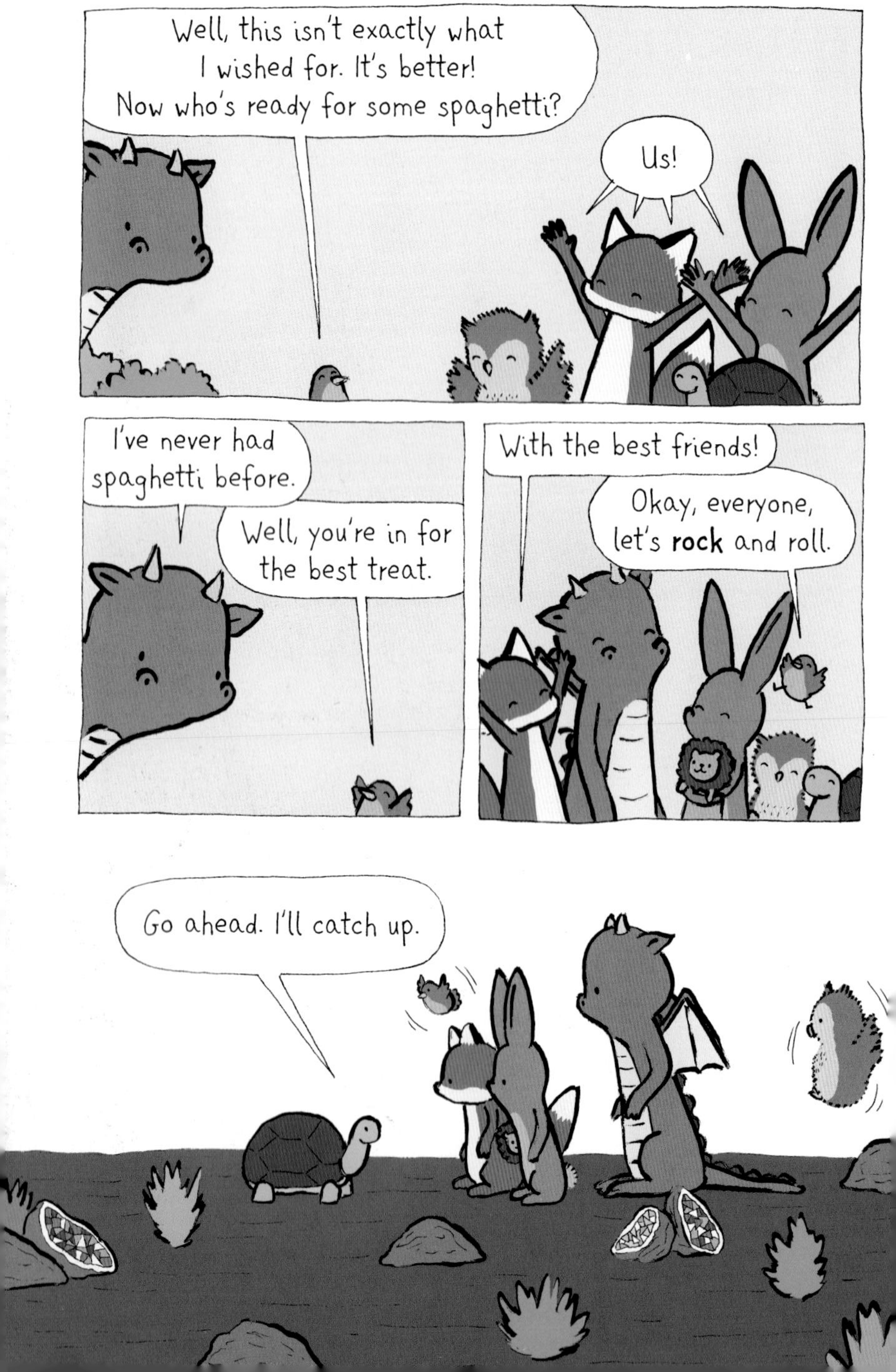
Well, this isn't exactly what I wished for. It's better! Now who's ready for some spaghetti?
Us!
I've never had spaghetti before.
Well, you're in for the best treat.
With the best friends!
Okay, everyone, let's **rock** and roll.
Go ahead. I'll catch up.

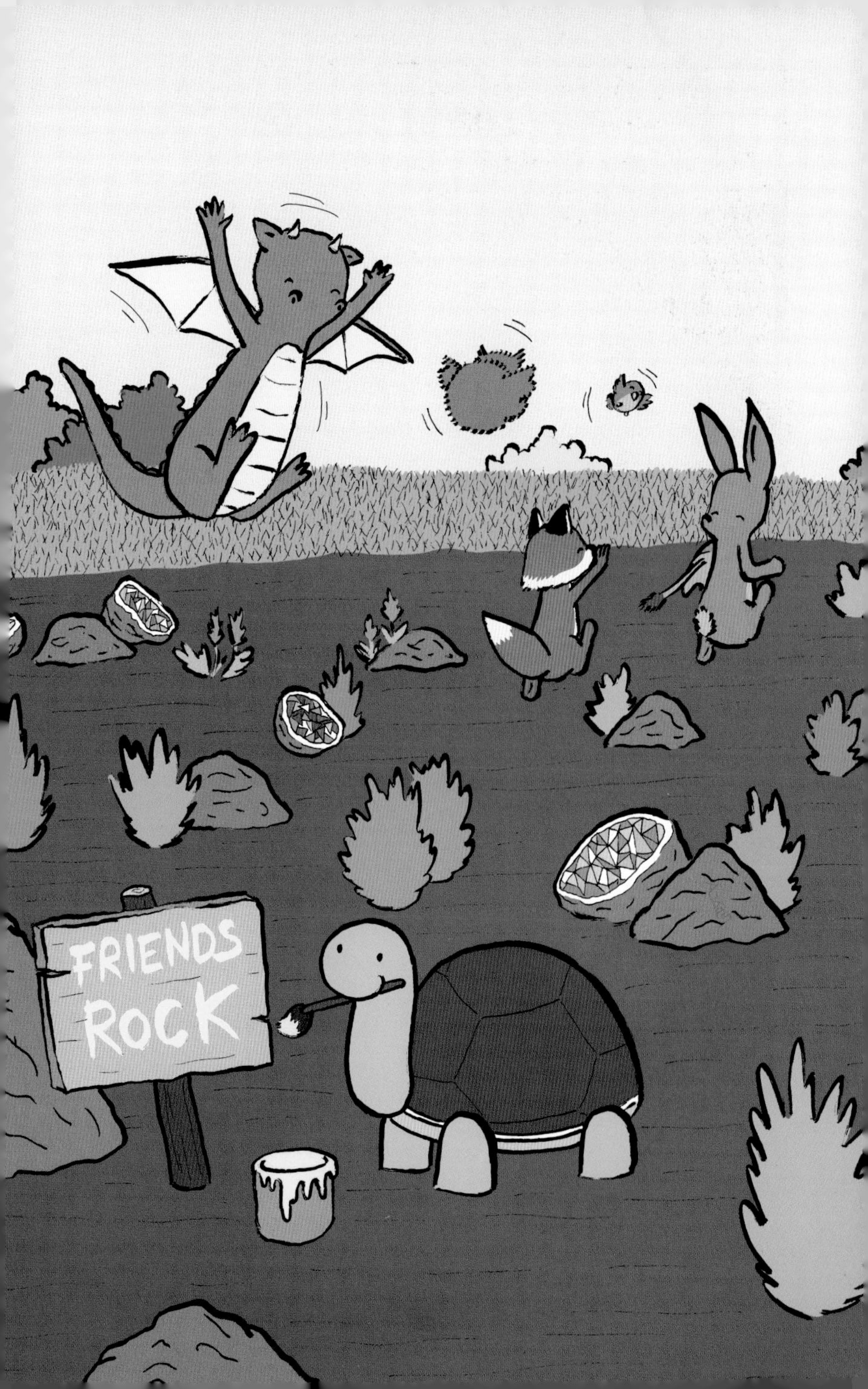
FRIENDS
ROCK

ABOUT THE AUTHOR

Beth Ferry celebrates the wonder of words and the magic of stories as the author of many books for young readers including the Fox & Rabbit series and myriad picture books illustrated by many talented artists. She lives by the beach in New Jersey where she celebrates summer and ice cream and friendship and reading and puppies and pizza and pumpkins. You can learn more at bethferry.com.

ABOUT THE ILLUSTRATOR

Gergely Dudás is a self-taught illustrator. He was born in July 1991. His artwork in the early 1990s was a lot more abstract than it is today. He is the creator of the Bear's Book of Hidden Things seek-and-find series.

Like Fox, Gergely likes fixing things. And like Sparrow, he loves celebrating, even the little things (for example, celebrating Sundays with crêpes). But unlike Rabbit, he doesn't know any dragons (yet).

He lives with his girlfriend and a dwarf rabbit called Fahéj.

Gergely's work is inspired by the magic of the natural world. You can see more from him at dudolf.com.

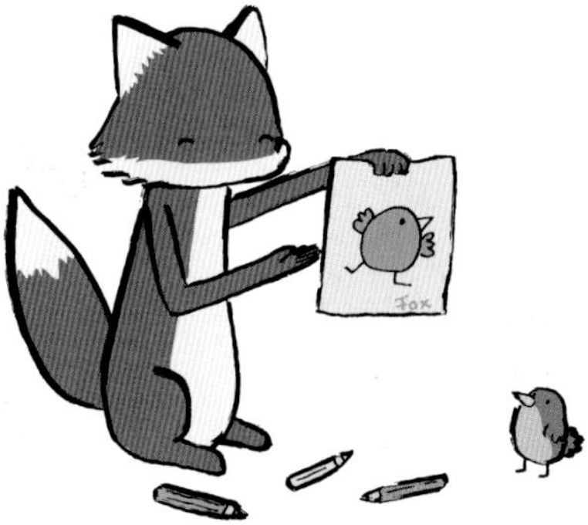
Fox

FOR JOSH, WHO GIVES US
SO MUCH TO CELEBRATE
—B.F.

FOR MY DEAR FRIEND VADI,
WHO APPRECIATES MY CHRISTMAS CARDS THE MOST
—G.D.

The art in this book was created with graphite and ink and colored digitally.

PUBLISHER'S NOTE: This is a work of fiction. Names, characters, places,
and incidents are either the product of the author's imagination or used
fictitiously, and any resemblance to actual persons, living or dead,
business establishments, events, or locales is entirely coincidental.

Library of Congress Control Number for the hardcover edition: 2020950724

Paperback ISBN 978-1-4197-4959-9

Text copyright © 2021 Beth Ferry
Illustrations copyright © 2021 Gergely Dudás
Book design by Heather Kelly

Printed and bound in China
10 9 8 7 6 5 4 3 2 1

Amulet Books are available at special discounts when purchased in quantity for premiums and
promotions as well as fundraising or educational use. Special editions can also be created to
specification. For details, contact specialsales@abramsbooks.com or the address below.

Amulet Books® is a registered trademark of Harry N. Abrams, Inc.

ABRAMS The Art of Books
195 Broadway, New York, NY 10007
abramsbooks.com